Learning How to Drown

Learning How To Drown

Collected Short Stories

Cat Hellisen

NewCon Press
England

First edition, published in the UK May 2018
by NewCon Press

NCP 157 (hardback)
NCP 158 (softback)

10 9 8 7 6 5 4 3 2 1

ISBN: 978-1-910935-81-1 (hardback)
978-1-910935-82-8 (softback)

Cover art by Les Edwards
Cover layout by Ian Whates

Edited by Ian Whates
Interior layout by Storm Constantine

Contents

Learning How to Drown

An Introduction

There's a tiny, hidden beach in Cape Town that was once, during the dark years of Apartheid, a private beach. These days it's open to the public but, because you need to know where it is and it's unmarked, the beach remains something of a locals' secret. While the tourist masses pay their fees to lounge on Boulders Beach, oohing and aahing as the penguins waddle from their sandy dens and out to the ocean, we locals pay nothing to swim through fronds of kelp, while fish and penguins flit below our feet; silvery ghosts in the murk haloed with a glittering aura of bubbles.

It might seem that this has absolutely nothing to do with writing, but since I have previously described my stories as tasting of iodine and salt water, or as gifts taken in a bucket from the sea, it might give you some picture of how I view stories and my place as a writer. Water – salt water, wild water, grey and green and icy water – seeps into my stories, fills up the spaces between the words.

I write stories about people who live on the edges. Sometimes on the literal edges where the ocean meets the land, but also about those people who don't fit into the world they've been given. They are mongrels and outcasts. Creatures 'neither fish nor fowl'. I once said they were 'fish out of water stories' but I think that's too simplistic a take. They are penguin-out-of-water stories. Like me, my characters are ungainly, odd-looking, strange-sounding creatures who clumsily make their way through the sandy dunes of human interaction. It's only when they hit water, when they dive into the ocean of words and dreams, that they become something… Other.

Stories are born in water, and I swim in dreams. Like penguins, and like my characters, I am momentarily free in the ocean. Oceans are not safe. They are huge and changeable and filled with monsters. Some so obvious that they are movie channel cliché. The Great Whites of narrative. Some awe us with their size, their almost human familial relationships. And some are small symbiotic monsters, floating innocently on the water surface while trailing stingers far below. My stories, these dreams I swim in, are likewise filled with monsters.

And just as penguins can't live their whole lives in the sea, I can't live there in my story ocean forever. I will always need to drag myself out of the water, my brain filled with ideas, and make my way back to this side.

This collection ranges from some of my earliest published stories – such as my take on a pirate Bluebeard and his last bride – to the very latest I've sold. Even those stories which were published a decade after my first are still tangled up in those kelp strand motifs. The images echo through the years, each story kissed by the one before, imparting brine and larval ideas. It soon became clear to Ian Whates while he was reading them that many of the stories centre around water, and it was he who suggested the final title *Learning How to Drown* instead of the rather less interesting title I had submitted the collection under. The new title could not be more perfect. It sums up how I write, what I write about, and what I want from the reader. I want you to learn how to drown with me, to immerse yourself and follow the monsters deeper.

Cat Hellisen
Fife
November 2017

The Girls Who Go Below

We practice drowning each other. It's the best way to spend summer, by Vera's lake (not Aunt Vera, she said. It made her feel old and she didn't like to be reminded, thank you, girls) where the sun slanted between the pale clouds like Zeus's own fingers to stroke the ripplewaves and stir them up.

We love the way water lies to us. From Vera's house it will look pewter-flat but as we tumble toward it, the water will shrug off its mirror face and turn amber and gold and brown and blue and filled with clouds and trees, like a gateway to another world.

Here at the edges. with our bare feet oozing into black and squishy cow-pat mud, the water will change again, grow red as sloe gin and suck at the roots of trees. It will be bottomless and filled with little fish-tremors, flicks of silver sides in the dark.

"This is the worst part," says Millicent. "The getting in." We sink, waiting for the right moment to slap forward into the froggy water, to where the big things live, all smooth and mysterious as monsters from the Jurassic oceans.

Vera says there are no monsters here, that the lake isn't big enough to support one, herbivorous or carnivorous. That we are safe.

We find that sadly boring. We want monsters. That's the fun of lakes and hollow black hills and forests deep and old as the bones of the Earth. They're supposed to be the homes of things we can't explain, otherwise what's the use of them?

Our feet are growing cold, mud oozing between our toes. Millicent steps forward first, splashing black slime in a perfect arc across the front of my knees. I bound after her, shoving and catching hands, and we screech and crow, our voices the only things to break the fat, summer-sweaty silence of the lazy morning.

The water is best once we are far out, floating on our backs. We hold hands so we don't drift apart. The lake is warm in patches, sun-heated, and every now and again we slip into a cold section, so surprisingly cold that it makes us believe we are not in a lake on a hillside farm under the looming Tsitsikamma mountains, but floating over nothingness, over an endless wellspring from which all things come. The damselflies skim past us, catching midges, oblivious to the monsters waiting yellow-eyed at our backs.

We drown in turns, holding each other under for longer and longer, counting out the seconds, waiting to see what will come first – the end of the countdown, or the manic flail that is our signal to stop drowning.

I'm gasping, head in the brightness, my eyes streaming with brackish tears, when Millicent stills next to me. Our legs and arms are entangled. We are as close as we've always been, but in that moment before she opens her mouth, I feel the snap that breaks us apart.

"Lucienne," she whispers, hot in my ear, making me shiver. "Who's that?"

We turn together, feet gently swirling, our bodies in layers of cold and warm and dark and amber, our hair serpenting around our throats, diamonds and rainbows in our eyelashes.

There is an invader on our bank, cross-legged calm, watching us from under the white milkwood. He raises one hand.

We do not.

"We don't like him," I say.

"Yes we do, Lucy," Milly tells me. "He might be interesting."

"Oh." Milly lies on her bed, knees up, the pillow clutched in her arms like a lover. "We should invite him next time we go swimming."

I scowl. Vera says that he is the son of one of the neighbouring farmers, that he has been away at Rhodes University, studying "some arty rubbish." He has a name. Mallery. I think it is a foolish name, reminding me too much of Great Uncle Milo, but Millicent adores it. "Millicent and Mallery, isn't that hilarious?" she says.

The years between us never felt big, but Mallery is a wooden peg driven into a split pine. We are being pushed apart.

I wait for Milly to fall asleep before I creep out of the house and tumble like a blackguard through carrot ferns and Cape ivy, down the moonlit paths where the stones are bright as plucked-out eyes reflecting the stars.

The farm is not far, though no self-respecting English girl would travel there alone in the dark. Vera pointed it out to us when we – when

Millicent – asked, and even in the dark the way is easy, my feet leading me sure as can be. Only when I reach the farmhouse door and see between the curtains that blue ghostly flicker of the television, hear the laughter, and taste sour peat in the air, do I think perhaps I am the one being foolish.

After all, Mallery is just a boy. Millicent has seen boys before, has drawn their initials in her diary and trapped them in closed-circuit hearts. I know all these things. I don't need to keep a diary. Milly's is enough for me.

So why am I upset by Mallery's coffee-ground eyes and the curling snare of his hair? Do I think that perhaps this time it is Millicent in danger of being caught, and not the other way around? Millie always lets them go, after all.

I wait on the wide farm stoop, wondering. Night has fallen with a cold wind, and I am dressed only in my nightdress and summer gown, my feet bare. Just as I'm about to turn and go back to my sister and to sleep, the door opens, and the boy intruder is staring at me, frowning.

"Hi," he says, confusion all slow and sweet on his tongue. "You're one of the Stephenson girls."

I stare at him.

"From the lake. Vera Notley's nieces, am I right?"

"No." I hold my head straight and high. "You're wrong. And stay away from our lake. And from us."

He calls out after me as I leave. "Wait." His feet thud soft, like a hunting dog, and then he is beside me. I pretend to ignore him. "It's not your lake," he says, huffing as he walks. I have long legs, a quick stride, I am sure-footed in the dark. "It's public land."

"I don't care what you think," I tell him. "You are invading our privacy."

He stops, and I turn to look back at him against my better judgement. "Ah, is that it."

"Is what it?"

"Nothing." He smiles at me, white fangs under the fat moon, and he raises his hand again. It's not a greeting, or a good-bye. He is saluting me. "Challenge accepted."

"There's no challenge –" But he is gone. I blink, and after a moment, go back to Vera's grand old wooden house, to my bed and my dreams. But it's impossible to fall asleep. My feet are burning as though

I walked through a field of crushed glass, and the feeling works its way up my legs and my belly and the hollow space meant for my heart, and the dreams I do have are hot and sharp like bottles broken at the edge of a fire.

It rains for three days and we use the time to practice our music. Mother has always pointed out that we are English ladies, and we shall have a Classical education and know our Heras from our Aphrodites, and play an instrument, and walk very prettily. I think she plans for us to go back to England, though I do not know how we can return to a place we have never been. Milly sings, trilling up and down scales, holding her position just so, while I play a dutiful piano accompaniment. My technique is very good, very precise. Our old teacher used to tell us that I was all slick perfection with no heart, which we thought was a terribly stupid thing to say. A piano is wires and wood and dull teeth. There's no place in machines for wet lumps of meat.

Milly bounces through our song, every crotchet and quaver, while the rain veils the hills, makes a thick curtain of moving dark and light across the glass. We perform for Vera, who drinks a port like watered blood and claps in delight when we are done. Milly smiles small, acknowledging her talent, and presses one hand to her neck, her fingertips just touching her earlobe. She's wound her golden hair up like an adult, but there are still streaks of sun-bleached white and those are not grown-up at all. Grown-ups do not play in the sun and pretend to drown their sisters.

We neither of us mention Mallery. Instead, we sing along to old swing records that buzz and crackle and jump on Vera's turntable, we take over the front parlour with a world map puzzle that is longer and wider than both of us. There are whales spouting in the oceans, and tigers prowling through India. It is lovely. It smells of cardboard. A sweet nutty smell like something might grow from it if we were to water the world.

But soon the sun is back, scattering butterfly-white wings across the rolling greens, and everything is perfumed damp and sweet and clean and when Milly kicks my feet and says, "We can't stay inside all day," I know that we are going back to the sloe gin lake.

There's no sign of Mallery by the shore, and perhaps this is good, he has understood he cannot take my sister from me. It's only when we are waist-deep in the water and spinning each other in circles, hands clasped, fingers tight and white, that we hear the sobbing.

Sweet and high, it throbs across the water and we still, the water hushing around us, pushing and lapping. We rock in place.

"What's that?"

I twist my mouth in annoyance. It's not as though we have never heard a violin before.

The music rises out of the tree line that stands a little distant from the lake. From the milkwood and yellowwood forest that crawls up the slopes, draping them in rustling shivery green.

"We should ignore it," I say. "Or go home."

Milly pulls her hands out of mine and wades to shore.

After a moment, I unstick my feet from the grabbing mud and follow her, the silt from her steps clouding around me, swirling like underwater storms. Something slides underfoot, eel-fast, and is gone.

Mallery is standing in the shadows of the ancient trees, his violin tucked under his chin. He doesn't even look at us until he has finished playing, then he lowers his instrument and stares at us as if he has called us here, little water beasts entranced by Orpheus's lyre.

Millicent hasn't bothered to throw a towel around herself, and the breeze has teased her cold. She stands, dripping and smiling, her sun-white streaks as bright as her teeth, her skin pale gold, like a palomino kelpie. I tuck my borrowed olive-green towel over my swimsuit and keep my distance. My skin has also been sun-dusted, but I take after our mother and, like her, am a shadow behind the sun.

"Mallery!" Milly smiles for him, waves. "That was beautiful. Aunt Vera –"

"Just Vera," I say.

"– Vera says you're from –" She pauses to shake topaz from her hair. "Delchik Farm." She unleashes her first weapon and smiles quickly, just once.

I sigh and roll my eyes.

"And that you're at Rhodes – is that what you're studying – music?"

"It's a hobby," he says. "Are you enjoying the lake?"

"Oh, yes. It's lovely, simply beautiful here." She turns to look back at me, wriggles her fingers, beckoning. "This is my sister Lucy –"

"Lucienne."

Her smile doesn't falter. "And I'm Millicent, but god, that is such a dreadful name, so I insist you call me Mill."

"Mill." He nods in greeting, and then to me, because we have never met. One time in the dark doesn't count. "Lucienne." Mallery holds his violin before him like a lovely breakable shield, and the fragile javelin of his bow dangles from his fingers. "I'm actually here to deliver a message."

Millicent – Mill – lets herself frown just the slightest. "A message. For us?"

"You're invited to dinner," he says. "Tonight, if that suits. You and your aunt."

We make plans – Millicent makes plans while I watch, and Mallery gets caught on the hooks of her fingers, tangled in the bleached-white web of her drying hair. Even though there is a space between them, I can already see the ghost of it happening.

"It's not really suitable, dears," says Vera when we tell her about the invitation. Her eyes are cloudy, worried.

"Oh, but why, it's perfectly respectable – you're going with us, after all," Milly says, a pout waiting to form. I know the tiniest twitches of her mouth, what each one means.

"It's not about that." Vera frowns. "The Delchiks are a strange lot." She means unsuitable. Mother wants us to marry well, or not at all, like Dearest Aunty Vera.

"Isn't everyone out in the country?" Milly waves her insult away almost as soon as she says it. "Not you, of course, Vera dearest, but most of them."

"They are not –" She sighs. "Fine. It's all just rumour, anyway."

I'm intrigued now, for the first time. I look up from the terrible sampler I've been mangling. "What rumours?"

"Oh, nonsense stuff, that the Delchiks have fairy blood, witch blood. That they can trick a person out of their money and land and mind – it's supposedly why they have the nicest bit of farmland in the whole area. Nonsense, of course. You're right. Utter country rubbish, fuelled no doubt by jealousy." She smiles too brightly. "We'll need to find you something to wear, Millicent. Those dresses of yours are getting outgrown."

Dinner is dark, filled with meat and wine. I am allowed a glass; Vera says sixteen is a perfectly acceptable age to begin the path to alcoholism, and Mallery fills my glass with tarry red wine from Franschhoek that I have to sip at and pretend to like. Millicent drinks as though she was born to it, and for the first time I wonder how much of my sister I don't know. Her thin fingers are tight around the stem of the glass, waiting to break it, as if it's a rose she wants to take home and press between family Bibles.

Vera insists Milly sing after dinner and Mallery's parents, who look as normal and unwitchy as is possible, are eager to hear my sister's famous voice. We are settled before the piano, Milly resting one hand on my shoulder so that we strike the perfect tableau: her in a burgundy dress I have never seen before, myself in my forest-green Sunday velvet, my brown hair pulled back into a child's ponytail. We are only a few measures into the piece when the violin sweeps in soft and slow, and Milly's voice soars with it. I strike an off note, and the sound of it reverberates in my head, drowning out the rest of the music.

Milly's fingers dig into my shoulder.

"You were off tonight," she says afterwards.

"I need fresh air. The wine." I leave her alone with the Delchiks and Vera, and step out onto the wide stoop, trying to breathe deep and catch again the feel of Milly and I perfectly in time and in tune. It's fading. A dream. Unreal.

The air here is pine-tinged, sharp as shards of falling mirrors, and I take in lungfuls of it, wondering why it feels as if I can't remember how to breathe. The front door clicks, and I hang on to the stoop rail and wish I could grow into the smooth dead wood. I do not want to talk to anyone now.

"She's very good," says Mallery.

"Go away."

"So are you."

"But I have no heart," I finish for him.

He moves behind me, shadow-slipping over the wood boards. From the forests, the bushpigs squeal. "I wouldn't say that."

That makes me turn. "I have always been told I have no heart."

Mallery shrugs. He's lit a hand-rolled white cigarette and the bright cherry of it sweeps through the dark, a little fire fairy. "Maybe you hid it so it could never be broken."

I laugh. "No."

But he carries on, and I might as well not have spoken. "You cut out your heart and hid it inside a... inside a little girl's music box – the type that plays a terrible plinking tune and spins a pink ballerina when it opens."

Milly has a box like that. I do not. But I listen.

"Then you took the box and hid it inside a shoebox filled with the love letters of people long-dead, and placed that inside a lead-lined chest, and locked it with thirty locks, before rowing out to the middle of the lake and dropping the chest overboard, where it sank to a place no one could ever reach." He sucks on his flat cigarette and blows out snaky smoke, then grins. "How did I do?"

"Awfully," I tell him. "There were thirty-one locks." I leave him, run back to my sister.

"Mallery makes his own violins," Milly tells me. "Can you believe that?"

"I don't care." I put a missing piece into Siberia and pick up another. I have been saving all the palest puzzle pieces for last, like icing on a cake.

It is not raining, but we are not swimming. Milly is waiting for Mallery to come fetch her – he's driving her into town so she can do some shopping. She wants a new dress. I'm invited but I do not want to go. "Go drive with idiot Mallery and the two of you can shop all day. I don't care."

Milly flicks the piece out of my hand. "You are in a beastly mood, Lucy. Beastly. I don't know what's got into you." She uncurls, stands, smooths her beautiful skirt down. "Well, I'm going. Don't say I didn't ask you."

After she's gone, I take my towel down to the lake and practice drowning myself. It's not as much fun. I let out slow, silvery streams of bubbles and try to tell my future in their constellations. Nothing. I dive for my heart, fingers combing through years of settled mud, but all I do is cloud the water and scare the frogs and leave the water filthier than when I got in. I have to shower twice to get the stickiness off my skin.

Vera has gone with Milly and Mallery, and I drift through her empty, lonely house, peering under the claw-footed furniture.

It is full of places to hide a heart, but I cannot find mine anywhere.

The first night Mallery visits me, Milly is asleep, snoring softly against the pillow she holds as close to her as she used to hold me. He comes to my window and I open it against my better judgement. He sits on the ledge and grins, legs swinging.

"What do you want?" I ask him. We are on the second floor. I could shove him off and listen for the crack and the snap. And the screaming, I suppose, if he didn't die clean.

"Why didn't you want to come with us?"

"Us?" There is no us. There was once, but Mallery was never part of my Us. "Go away," I say. "Before you wake my sister."

He kisses me before he goes, and it tastes like the bloody red heart I cannot find. It tastes small and lonely.

Milly twirls for me, dancing on demi-pointe, the wings of her new dress curling about her thighs. In the long mirror, her reflection dances and the ivory dress drapes her like liquid bones.

"So." She flops next to me on my bed.

I stop chewing on the end of my pencil and close the little diary I have begun. "So what?"

"What do you think?"

"Of?"

She pokes my shoulder. "The dress, stupid." She leans over and I can smell the wine and mint chewing gum on her breath, sour and sharp. "What's this you're writing then?"

"Nothing."

"So do you think Mallery will like the dress?"

"I suppose."

She hums to herself as she holds earrings against her cheeks, discarding this one and that one. I frown. She's off-key. Milly knows this piece as well as she knows the angles and planes of her own face – she would usually correct herself immediately if she went even the slightest bit flat.

It digs into my eardrums like the morning screeching of the hadeda ibis flocks and I will my sister to go, to take her tuneless happiness away from me.

When she leaves, I erase all the words I have written until they are just faint scratches on the paper, ghost writing, ghost dreams. I write a new diary over the old; inconsequential nonsense and I like that, because I can remember the bones of what I wrote underneath, like fossils. I smile and obliterate my dreams of Mallery, of finding my heart in the lake mud and playing a perfect piano, singing a song better and brighter than anything Milly can do. Could do.

This is how the summer holiday passes. I learn to keep secrets from my sister, and she grows a new life that doesn't include me. At night, when she is dreaming, I slip through the house and meet Mallery by the peaty beach, and we stand barefoot in the cold black water and count the ripples of moonbreath on the skin of Vera's lake, listen to the screaming things. He tells me he has seen the elephants in the forest pass by like ghosts, and I tell him he is a liar, that they are all dead.

"The forest is full of things that people say don't exist."

We kiss until I learn what a heart tastes like.

"You're not like your sister," Mallery says, but I cannot tell if that is meant to be a compliment or a critique.

I straighten, turn away from him, my arms folded across my chest, cradling the things I feel and keeping them safe.

Mallery touches the back of my neck. "I would like to hear you sing."

"So you can see which of us is better?" I shift away from him, shrug off his touch.

"Maybe," he says, but he laughs as he does and I know he has already chosen.

"Milly thinks that you're in love with her." I tell him, though he already knows this. "And that she's in love with you."

"Millicent is capable of thinking many things, not all of which I agree with."

Finally, I turn to look at him. He's thoughtful, brow crinkled softly. I think of forests, of wild things, of ghost animals. Of the gleam of moonlight and kisses until the shadow of my sister slides between us. I frown.

"Would you like to see how I make a violin?" Mallery asks.

The perfect violin needs the right material, and even then the luthier needs to work with that material, shape it so that it can sing the song inside itself, its heart. Mallery tells me this, and explains what he needs.

"She'll be beautiful, you'll see," he says. "But it takes time, preparation."

I nod. My fingers itch, my throat is dry with want. I cannot speak. My lungs have filled with a strange fluid, like drowning in sloe gin and honeyed wine. When Mallery smiles at me, I think of witch blood, of fairy blood.

"She's not what she used to be, is she?" Mallery whispers to me as he holds me closer. His whispers curl around me, tight as threads.

She's not my sister any more, that much is true. But Mallery made her that way. Didn't he?

Didn't he?

She was supposed to trap his name in an ink heart and then forget about him. As she always does. It's Milly who changed. Not me. Not anyone else. She broke the rules.

"I can make her the same as she was," Mallery says. "Give her back her voice."

On the last day of summer I drown the thing that used to be my sister. I count out the seconds in silvery bubbles, past her flailing hands.

When she is still and quiet, Mallery cuts a lock of her sun-bleached hair with a pair of my embroidery scissors. He curls Milly's hair up into a tight little noose, wraps it in his handkerchief, then tucks it back into his shirt pocket. I am a little jealous of that intimacy; her palomino hair embraced in monogrammed cotton, pressed close to his heartbeat.

We weight the body with stones before we push the corpse down. The lake bed is a sludgy mess of drowned trees and silt so deep that Millicent's body will be swaddled away, waiting for us to return. I mark where the body goes below, or I'll never find her. Then I wipe the shallow grazes on my arms clean, and stare at them. She didn't fight us very much. The thing that was my sister knew it had to drown.

Although I know I lost her when summer started, I find myself sobbing. Mallery says nothing to my grief, just watches me crouch at the edge of the lake, my legs black with mud, my tears salting the water.

Next summer I go back to Vera's lake alone, one half of Us. I have cried myself out, emptied the space inside, ready to find my heart in the dark. I told my story over and over, that I did not see her go into the lake, that she was meant to meet me, and never turned up. Divers came all the way from George to search the lake, but found nothing, and the police soon turned their attention to the forests, and to the workers who lived on the neighbouring farms

Vera is sombre-faced, older than she likes to pretend she isn't. "Oh, darling," she says. "Are you sure?"

I'm wearing my bathing togs, a borrowed towel slung over one shoulder. "I have to," I tell her. "Do you understand?" And then in a whisper. "I have to."

She doesn't tell me to be careful, just cries silent tears that fall down her cheeks like slow worms. But she nods, because I suppose she thinks she understands.

I meet Mallery by the water's edge and we dive in the place where we sank Milly, holding our breath until it feels as if we are drowning, our fingers carding through the mud.

I'm the one who finds her, cushioned and pillowed and blanketed in her lake-bed. We pull up the clumps of her that we can use and afterwards I sit on the bench in Mallery's workshop and watch him as he whittles and carves her breastbone into a violin neck, makes tuning pegs from her knuckle bones. He strings her hair on the bow, rosins it ready, and it is perfect, so beautiful, just like my sister.

When she's ready, Mallery plays for me, and the strings weep under the white-bleach hair of the bow. I listen to my sister sing, sweet and filled with her sobbing. Then he lowers his bow, tucks the golden violin into the crook of his arm, and waits for my reaction.

"Oh," I say. "Bow and balance me." I take the violin from him and set it on my shoulder, tuck it under my chin. Mallery comes to stand behind me, correcting my grip on the bow, and when I slide my sister's taut-pulled hair across the gut strings, the first long, sweeping note throbs in my chest.

I'm often inspired to do modernish retellings of fairy tales and folk songs, which then veer off course and end up barely resembling the source material. "The Girls Who Go Below" was one of these. It was inspired by Martin and Eliza Carthy's rendition of The Bows of London *with its sister murderer and the tell-tale violin made from her bones and hair, but set in a world I knew: the forests of Knysna.*

WAKING

The Museum of Angelic Artefacts was a roadside attraction; a blip on the map where families stopped to stretch their legs and maybe take in an old film of the visitations. They would round out their break with a trip to the shops to buy coffee and ice cream, a postcard to put in a drawer and forget.

It wasn't a big museum, as these things go. Most of the display was of small mechanical pieces; cogs and electrodes and bits of broken chips. A few whole metal skeletons were in the main display at the back of the house, and they were the pieces that drew the biggest crowds. The bio-parts of the angels were harder to find, although we did possess a small glass-topped trunk with an embalmed hand that was supposed to have come from one of the first angel visitations. Of course, there are fingers of Gabriel in several museums.

The last of the angels' visitations ended before my parents were born. There are newsreels showing the first landings, gritty and sepia and jerkily out of time. The angels were taller than the people clustered around them, but they weren't scary or anything.

They just stood there, blinking. No celestial messages of deliverance, no words from distant stars. After a while, they died. Fell apart. The visitations became so common that scientists identified over five-hundred types, and catalogued them all. We like to catalogue things, even if we don't know why. Order.

We gave them names and ranks. It started as a joke – cherubim and seraphim, Michael and Uriel. The names lost meaning. Hard not to when there are hundreds of Gabriels.

Eventually we stopped caring. An angel would arrive, alone, would stand uselessly still, and finally crumple to its knees with a sad dusty crash.

The labs kept a few alive on life support for a while, but it didn't really make any sense in the long term. They switched off the last of them, CB #7 1397/168-sph, a few weeks ago. It was about three months before my seventeenth birthday, and I wouldn't even have known about the angel if it hadn't been the kind of thing my parents keep track of for the museum. They printed out the little article and put it up on the notice board to be ignored along with everything else.

I noticed that display #394 had disappeared because it was my job to Windex all the glass each morning, while Mom ran the office and tried to keep my baby brother's screams from waking the whole neighbourhood, and Dad took the morning deliveries. On weekends we had help in the form of Elliot the Boy Wonder, so named because it was a wonder he came to work, considering how much pot he smoked.

The hand in the display had been very neatly taken – no broken glass or jimmied locks, so I went looking for Camelia.

She wasn't in the back yard where the wreck of a 27-oph stood, like a giant hamster wheel slowly turning to rust.

"Cam?" The back fence, half-hidden behind a scraggly hedgerow of blackjacks and rosemary, had a torn section that Cam could fit through. Me too, if I crawled on my belly and didn't mind getting mud all over my front, and black jacks in my hair. "Cam, you idiot," I said to myself and knelt to peer through the gap. I didn't need to look for clues. Of course she took the hand.

My parents moved from the city to Meriphem when I was five, so I don't really remember much of what came before. My sister was one, a fat squalling nightmare, and the car trip was a mash of spilled cold drink gone sticky on the back seat leatherette, my mother's eyes wobbly with tiredness, my father driving with the window open so that cold air sluiced over us, and, like a generator powering us further and further away from the city tower blocks, my sister's wail.

They'd left behind their city jobs and bought a house filled with junk, with the tiny parts and empty corpses of angels. And they'd turned it into a business. There was a museum and little tea shop and curio shop where visitors could buy paintings of angels that looked nothing like real ones.

I should have told Mom and Dad when we found our angel. But that would have meant explaining what we were doing out in the little forest that edged the town, instead of being at school. Cam was twelve, so I guess she could have maybe cried her way out of it, but at sixteen I wouldn't have had an excuse, and everyone said the second-last year of school was actually the most important and if you failed *that* your life might as well be over.

Mine already was, as far as I could see. My parents had been saddled with the late miracle of Ivan, Cam was making a name for herself as some kind of violin prodigy, and I was doing nothing more exciting that getting mediocre grades and cleaning glass cases in a house full of dead angels.

"Cam?" I called again as I crashed through the little narrow deer trails that spread through the forest like veins and arteries through a sweltering heart. I found her exactly where I'd expected, sitting cross-legged in front of the angel.

"What are you doing here?" I asked. The hand was laid out on a maroon velvet cloth in front of her; an offering to the silent remains of an enigma. "Mom and Dad will kill you when they see that."

Cam's head turned like it was on a wire and she stared at me in that slow unblinking way she had when she was thinking deeply about something. "They won't actually kill me," she said eventually.

"It's an expression." I sidled closer and glanced at the angel. It looked the same as it had the day before. And the day before that and the day before that. I don't know why we kept coming back. It was about a head shorter than me and it wasn't new or anything, or alive. It just was. "Why did you bring it the hand?"

She shrugged. This wasn't the first time Cam had brought it a gift. Only last week she'd carried her violin case all the way here to play for the angel. She'd kept to the more uplifting pieces. But she'd never brought it an actual physical offering before. The hand was a new development. "It doesn't have one of its own."

The angel didn't have much of its own, to be honest. The parts of it that hadn't rotted away had been exposed to air for too long, and the metal had turned a strange unearthly blue. The trunk was still solid, and the mechanised joints of its base skeleton were still there. The feet and arms and head were gone, along with any skin it might once have had.

"It's dead." I touched her shoulder. "Come on, Cam, put the hand back before anyone notices. Leave the angel."

"It needs a hand." She shook her head, the dark curls streaming like they were caught in a storm. But she clambered to her feet. "It asked me for one."

My back prickled with sweat, and I pulled the front of my tee-shirt away from my chest. "Angels don't talk, they never have."

"This one does." Cam folded the hand in its velvety shroud and followed me back to the museum.

Weekends we were supposed to help out at the museum, or, if we couldn't do that, at least help Mom with Ivan so she could have a break from his incessant screeching.

"I hate him," Cam said, and glared at the demon lying in the pram, his fists and face scrunched up like paper full of angry words.

"You don't hate him," I told her in a flat voice, and jiggled the pram a little harder as we walked together down the road. A few joggers and parents out with their kids gave me disapproving stares. "Hate is a very strong word." I thought about all the things I was supposed to feel, and how I didn't really understand them. I didn't hate Ivan, but I didn't love him either. He was just an annoyance. I didn't have a passion for music like Cam did. I didn't even feel much about the knowledge that Elliot the Boy Wonder like-liked me, beyond thinking it weird.

Ivan paused in his screaming, probably to psych himself up for another round.

"You don't know what I feel," Cam said. "And I am a very strong person. And strong people have space only for the strongest emotions. Like hate."

"Or love," I countered, before glancing over at her. "Anyway, you were just as bad." My blurry memories of my childhood always came back to me wrapped in cobwebs like forgotten presents. Maybe that's why I never really felt much of anything.

Cam snapped out of her frown, her face flowering curious. "Was I? How did you manage not to murder me?"

"I almost did," I said. It was a strange confession to make, I hadn't thought about that night in years, but Ivan's screams had brought the memory back to me with an unusual clarity. It made me uncomfortable to remember. I'd felt too much. "You'd actually stopped crying for a bit, but it didn't matter because you'd kept me awake all night anyway."

"How old was I?"

From the depths of the pram, Ivan's wail began, slowly growing in intensity like an air raid siren. I raised my voice. "Two, I think? You must have been, you were still in your cot, but you weren't in Mom and

Dad's room." The edges of that night were knife-blue, slicing up through the fog I lived in.

"What happened?"

Instead of facing her, I bent over the handrail of the pram as if I were checking Ivan. I remember doing the same thing that night. Standing on tip-toe in my teddy-bear nightie, my legs needle-cold, toes numb. The wooden rail of the cot digging into my stomach. Camelia sleeping. Not pudgy and content – that was never her way. She was thin and strange even then, and I thought oh it would take nothing now to make you stay quiet like this forever. I even took the yellow blanket that she'd kicked off, and folded it over and over and pressed it down over her face.

She would have died quietly. Maybe my parents wouldn't have had another child. No whine of Cam's violin when she practised a new piece, no screeching from Ivan as he shared his constant rage at the world. Passion was loud. It deafened everyone else in the world, pushed them under.

"Nothing," I said, and skated Ivan's pram faster down the sidewalk. "Obviously. So if I could live though the horror of you, you can live through the horror of Ivan. Fair's fair."

That week I went to the angel on my own every day after school. Mom and Dad had signed Cam up for a slew of extra violin lessons. While she had a middle-aged gentleman watching her with bleary eyes to make sure she stood exactly so, and played exactly such, I met with the angel.

The little glade it was in always seemed more peaceful than the rest of the town, even more peaceful than the surrounding forest. The sounds of the birds and rabbits became distant, as easily forgotten as the far-away drone of the highway. It was an oasis of quiet. I would take off my regulation socks and shoes, use my regulation school blazer to sit on, and work on my regulation studies. There was a sweet and simple rightness to it.

No screaming, no tourists, no child-genius little sister, no Elliot the Boy Wonder trying to stare at my tits between tours, no interruptions. I would get a lot more studying done in those two hours a day than I would manage the rest of the entire week.

On Wednesday I discovered that Cam and I were not the only ones who knew about the angel. I stepped into the glade, already smiling at how calm the place was, and stopped. Sunlight fell in soft threads through the leaf canopy, highlighting the damaged struts, the toxic blue of the eroding metal.

Someone had left a plastic bag in front of the angel. The bag stank sweetly, and a few lazy fat greenbottles crawled over and into the plastic crevasses, their buzzing amplified. It sounded like a million tiny aeroplane engines trapped in a cold drink can.

"Ugh." Trying to touch the entire thing as little as possible, I managed to untie the packet. Inside was half a sheep's head and two jointed pig's trotters, both still in their cling wrap, with the price on. Cheap meat cuts from the butcher's. Gagging, I tied the bag closed and hunted around for a place where the ground was soft enough to bury it.

I had to dig the hole with a broken branch, and I moved the bag by using the same stick to catch the loops and carry it. The meat made a solid dead sound, and the patter of soil after was like the rain falling on newly planted seeds. The flies dispersed, taking their unwelcome hum away, back out into the world.

With the offering buried, I didn't want to stay. After all, what kind of weirdo brings body parts to a dead angel? Besides my sister. There was no way it could have been her. She was still in school, a prisoner.

But what if it was her? She'd brought it the hand, she said it spoke to her. I needed to make sure.

So I stayed, half-focusing on my studies, half-watching the leaves and branches wavering around me, the sun haloing everything in gold dust. But no one came, and evening fell in long feathery shadows that painted the husk of the angel in alternating deep indigos and flame oranges

Wings

I thought as I left.

I need wings.

That evening, over the screaming and the blare of the news, I tried to ask Cam about the sheep's head and the pig trotters, but my tongue swelled up and stuck to the roof of my mouth.

All night I dreamt of flying.

By breakfast time my tongue had gone back to normal, and while Mom walked Ivan round in desperate little circles, and we ate our corn flakes, I asked Cam about the offerings.

My mother's heels tack-tack-tacked across the floor. A rubbish truck reversed up our road, beeping incessantly. Ivan grumbled, a low constant growl that was his sleepy precursor to his all-day screaming sessions.

"There were weird things out by the clearing," I said, keeping my voice soft enough to not compete with the rest of the noise.

"Weird things?" Cam raised an eyebrow, then shovelled another spoonful of yellow flakes and sugary milk into her mouth. The crunch was enough to drive me insane.

"Yeah. Meat. In a packet."

The bovine chewing continued for a while. Ivan began to whimper. My mother said; "Ssh, ssh, ssh," and jiggled him like a noxious water balloon she was afraid of bursting. It was starting. The whimper grew louder, higher pitched, the sound driving into our eardrums like diamond-tipped drills.

Cam stared at me before finally swallowing. "They weren't mine," she said in a low whisper. She needn't have bothered. It's not like Mom would be able to hear us over the shrieking. "Someone else must be able to hear it talking."

"It doesn't talk. It's a lump of rusting metal." If angels had ever tried to speak to us before, perhaps it was through their silences, and we – stupid loud buzzing things – had simply not understood. There were texts that said the true voices of angels were terrible to hear. Maybe humanity was simply scared of facing a quiet world, a terrible silence. So instead of listening to the nothings of angels, we jabbered at them, prodded them, filmed them, attached them to clanking, wheezing machines.

No wonder they died.

We hadn't taken the time to listen.

I left school after first period, faking menstrual cramps, and went to the clearing, back to Cam's angel. No one at school would even notice I was gone.

Whoever had brought the previous offering had come again, sometime between nightfall and late morning. An adult? Maybe. There was a new offering now – a stuffed toy cat, one of those hyper-realistic ones that cost too much money. It was brown, the tail tipped with a black tuft like a paint brush. Not a house cat, but a lioness. The secret visitor had placed the stuffed lioness on one of the prongs that jabbed out from the top of the angel's body.

I touched the plush fur, stroking it gently, running my fingers from nose tip to tail tip. A soothing moment.

"This is mental," I said to the angel.

Wings it said back to me.

"Keep quiet."

It hadn't spoken. There was no head, no mouth, it was a piece of abandoned machinery. For all we knew it had never even been an angel in the first place. I was tired. I was tired.

Before I left, I put the piece of Angus steak I'd shoplifted in front of it.

"We should show Ivan the angel," Cam said. It was Saturday. We'd been handed the Terror so Mom could go help Dad with the museum.

Elliot was apparently sick, but I'd seen him last night when Dad and I had gone to get take-outs. He'd been half-drunk already, standing with a group of friends, all of them dressed in those fake angel wings you could buy for kid's parties. Elliot's eyes had been rimmed with black, his mouth painted. They'd raised their Styrofoam cups when we drove past and cheered, and I'd tried to sink as low in my seat as possible while balancing four milkshakes on my lap. I still managed to get strawberry pink drips all down my leg.

"No." I was pretending Ivan was an aeroplane. It was one of the few activities that kept him quiet for any length of time. It was also very tiring. "Wheee! Flying! Ivan's flying!"

"Why not?"

Because I didn't want to see if other people had found my angel, if there were more packets of meat or stuffed toys or whatever people had decided to bring it in offering. Because I didn't want it to see Ivan, and I didn't want to hear what it wanted next. "Because I'm not going crawling through the woods with a one-year-old." I made him balance on his little socked feet. "Walk!"

He stumbled eagerly along, my hands under his armpits. Then he laughed.

It was so unexpected that neither Cam nor I could say anything for a moment. We just stared at each other blankly, as if we couldn't understand the sound he'd made.

"He'd like the angel," Cam said, just as Ivan gave up on his experimental laugh and launched into another full-bellowed roar.

Ivan screamed all that night, and we took turns with him. Mom rocked him, Cam played him lullabies on her violin, a sweet tragic sob. Dad drove him around the block a few times, and the momentary stillness was a balm laid across the entire house. We could all of us breathe easily until his return.

When I held Ivan, his fat bottom cradled on my arm, his fists in my hair, his breathless, hiccoughing mouth right by my ear, I remembered wanting to snuff Cam out. That long ago moment where I'd almost silenced her forever. I never felt like that with Ivan. I wanted to give him a voice, instead. If he could tell us what he wanted, if he could fly, maybe then he'd stop screaming.

"What do you want?" I asked him softly, but it was lost under a wail, the heat of his breath against my cheek, his tears damp on his sticky face, pressed against mine. "What do you want?" I asked but there was no one to hear me but the desiccated dusty remains of a thousand angels.

Ivan had another doctor's appointment on Monday. Maybe this one would find the switch, would work out what was wrong and give us a simple answer. Maybe Ivan felt too much where I felt too little. Perhaps there was a machine that could drain off the excess, feed his passion into me like a transfusion.

That night when Ivan finally cried himself to sleep, I dreamt of flying and laughing, and I woke to find myself in the clearing before the angel. It was painted by moonlight and shadow, in every shade of blue and silver. Tied together with strands of hair from Cam's violin bow were three sparrows. They were still alive, fluttering and chirring in terror. The flaxen horsehair was knotted around a spur of metal, keeping the little russet sparrows captive.

I stood barefoot in the dew-wet clearing, moon-anointed, and snapped the hairs strand by strand, while the sparrows beat at me with their little wings, pecked and clawed.

One died. The other two flew off into the night, and I dreamed my way back home.

A voice, said the voiceless angel.

While Mom was at church and the rest of our family enjoyed our atheism by reading or sleeping, Ivan went missing. It might not have been a holy day, but it was the only day the angel museum was closed, so it was pretty sacred to the rest of us.

I'd been studying, which actually meant I'd being lying on my bed with my textbook draped over my face. I woke only because the house was so eerily quiet that I heard the bells ringing. I was exhausted from another night full of Ivan's keening, strange dreams, of swollen silence, beating wings and the smell of wet earth.

"Alissa." My dad's voice, sleep-addled and sick. He always sounded sick, thanks to Ivan. Ivan who never stopped screaming, even though phalanxes of doctors had told my parents that there was nothing physically wrong with him.

"Mmm?" I sat up, the text book falling to my lap with a heavy thump. "I was studying –"

"Do you know where your sister and Ivan are?"

Terror iced over me, freezing my joints stiff. "No." I made myself swallow, stand, set my biology textbook on my little study desk. Normal things. "She must have taken him for a walk."

"You think so?" He was frowning. His shirt and face were rumpled, like he'd been taken out of the laundry and left to wrinkle. "Maybe. I didn't hear her leave."

"I'll find them." I dug my slops out of my cupboard and tried to smile. "Don't worry."

I took the short cut; through the museum and under the back fence. I'd stopped only to check the case for #394 and, as expected, the Gabriel Hand was also gone. I ran most of the way to the angel's clearing, my heart thudding in my ears, driving me on. There was no screaming, the forest was heavy and dense, the sounds swallowed up and muffled.

I found them in the clearing, Cam on her knees, feet tucked neatly under, sun brown heels bare. Elliot was leaning against one of the trees, smiling beatifically, drunkenly. He had a bottle of whiskey cradled in his lap. The previous night's make-up had been rubbed off, but around his eyes there were still smudges of black. He looked like a fallen angel in one of the paintings. Not like a real angel. The clearing smelled sweet and heavy; frankincense, myrrh, and marijuana.

"Hey, Alissa." Elliot raised his bottle in greeting, rich gold liquid sloshing around. It was more than half-gone. "Welcome to the wake. A wake. Awake. We're waking the angel."

"Ivan?" My breath came short and sharp; I could barely say his name. My heart clamoured and seized, screamed and filled with silence.

The clearing hummed, but my own breath was caught in my lungs and I couldn't force it out. I remembered the yellow blanket, the silence. How Cam grew up, and I didn't. Not inside, where it mattered. How Cam could feel things and all I had was the emptiness. How Ivan could fill the world with himself, and I drifted through the universe doing nothing but polishing glass and dreaming.

"Where is he?" I asked, just before I spotted him, small and terribly silent. His legs were wedged inside the body of the angel. Ivan stared at me, eyes wide, contemplative. Elliot's angel wings had been slipped over his arms. They were crumpled and dirty, and one of the feathers stuck out at an awkward angle.

"He's fine," said Cam. "Give him another anchovy. He likes those." She raised herself, and leaned forward, still on her knees, with something small and dark between her fingers. A tin of anchovies sat on the ground below her. Her violin case was next to it, unzipped and open, the maple shiny bright against blue velvet.

"What the hell is going on?"

Cam popped a sliver of tiny fish into Ivan's mouth. He ate it silently. That was not Ivan, screaming, red-faced Ivan.

"You should know," said Elliot. "You brought us here."

I looked down at the ground in front of the angel. The Ivan. There were the remains of one of the sparrows, the steak. Someone had dug out the packet with the sheep's head and the pig trotters and unwrapped them and set them out neatly. There was the toy lioness, Gabriel's Hand. A box of complimentary matches from the Museum of Angelic Artefacts.

"Thank you," said the Ivan. The voice was soft and adult. "For listening." It fluttered its party-wings experimentally, then, with a sound like tearing spider silk, it moved one articulated arm out to me. The sun glinted off the blue of the eroded metal, and outside the forest the bells called soft.

"Waking" is the closest I've come to writing out-and-out science fiction, though it's possibly only SF if you squint. It's a first contact story where humans have to learn to listen. Not just to the voices of otherworldly visitors, but to each other. A story about finding your place in family and in the larger world. It involves a hybrid transformation, which you'll see a fair amount of in my stories.

The Subtle Thief

It's the word that stops the world.

I was thirteen.

Now I'm sitting in a bar in New-Town, watching for the flicker. The Jump.

I was thirteen, and the world was a strange and wonderful place, a cup filled with fascination, overflowing to spill at my feet. Even the Fallen cities with their thorn barriers of barbed wire – even they beckoned. We weren't allowed there, of course, but the wires with their wrappings of flapping red ribbons called us closer.

There were tales told late at night about the Fallen cities, and we listened to them, our eyes big as ostrich eggs. Magic, our parents would whisper. There are things no man should do. Magic destroyed them. Incantations. Time after time. The dead cities stood as reminders of the power of words.

Come see, the ribbons said. Come see.

It was Jerry who followed them first, succumbed to the siren of rags flapping limply in the dry wind. It was always Jerry. Jerry and Mark and me. There go we three. We skipped school, leaving the dry rustle of paper and the bark of teachers for the sound of leaves and the feel of trees.

"We could go in," Jerry had said, pale under the innocence of little-boy freckles, so deceptive. "They'll never know."

"Of course they will." Sad fat Mark with his runny nose, the smears always silvery-fresh on his sleeve. So practical in his subservience and fear of the law, it was amazing that he followed Jerry around. Jerry seemed to tolerate him only for the unconscious amusement he provided. "There's alarms," he said. "If the metros get you, they'll lock you up forever – I've heard that they pull out all your fingernails and toenails, before they feed bits of you to their dogs."

We contemplated this information, comparing this potential pain with the reality of our limited childish experiences. I had ripped my toenail just the week before, and my little toe was a dark purple thing, bereft, and still tender.

"They do not."

Even as Jerry spoke we peered about us, wary as cranes, looking for the flash of sun against visor, ears open for the sound of barking. Only the constant shriek of the midday insects could be heard. Jerry shrugged, and beckoned toward the fluttering rags. "Besides, even if there was alarms once, there's nothing now. Right, Gaz?" He turned to me.

I was his lieutenant. I had to nod. "Yeah. It's all just stories."

"Right."

Satisfied, Jerry was already propping up the tangled wires with a rusty length of steel. Mark sighed, wiped the back of his pudgy hand across his face, and lumbered toward Jerry. I joined him.

Inside, the city wasn't asleep – but a dead thing, grey and leached. The bones of spires scraped the belly of the sky, but even they held no power. Drifts of rubbish had built up in the narrow alleys to create a thick and stinking compost. We wrinkled our noses.

Trees enclosed in neat little cages of square chain-link stood sentinel along the roads. Most were dead, so unlike the ones outside. A few held limp leaves up to the sky, little curled offerings. One fell at my feet, and I crunched it under my rubber sole.

"D'ya think anything still lives here?" Mark's voice wavered. Something scuttling in a tangle of plastic answered his question.

"Not people, really," said Jerry. "Just rats and things." I glanced down into the dark maw of a blocked alley. Shapes moved, hump-backed, through the rusted girders and blasted corpses of old-fashioned cars. We shifted back, as a unit, toward the open space of the road.

"Big rats," said Mark.

"You scared?" Jerry was all sneer and bluster, and of course, he got Mark every time. Before he could answer, Jerry had already taken off down the street, the heels of his trainers flashing white.

"Shit," I said, and ran after him, leaving Mark behind.

I lost them both that day.

Instead I found the word.

It was seven feet high, written on the side of a redbrick building with crumbling edges. It looked like it had been burnt in to the wall. A beautiful word, with soft shapes that shifted as I looked at them, with hard angles that clacked against one another.

I said it aloud.

And the world

stopped.

I found Jerry up ahead, frozen in place, grinning and maniacal, one foot poised to the ground like a dancer.

"Stop kidding around, Jer-boy," I said, and prodded at his shoulder. Immobile, he stood solid, balanced on the bent toe of his dusty trainer, the laces frayed and forlorn, trailing on the ground.

"Come on, Jerry, this isn't funny."

Still he stayed, and my heart beat as tightly against my ribs as a child's hand on a djembe. I backed away from him and looked slowly around, shivering under the summer sun. I could hear nothing in the distance – not the rasping shriek of locusts, nor the dim and faraway buzz of New-Town and her open-air spice markets.

All was still, and in the stillness I ran back to where Mark waited like a pudgy beacon. Sweat and bewilderment were frozen onto his red face. That the two were playing some incomprehensible practical joke on me seemed to be the most logical answer, but even all my shaking couldn't make Mark break from his pose.

Even the hunched rats were silent.

I panicked.

Finally, exhausted and frightened, I resorted to running between my two friends, trying not to think. They were only a few blocks apart and I travelled up and down, maybe four times, before the stasis released them, and the world went on as it always had. I said nothing to my friends, trapped as I was between my own disbelief that I had just managed to work some kind of ancient and forbidden magic, and the faint glimmer of my pride.

"I want to go home," Mark said.

For once Jerry didn't argue, as if he too felt the after-effects of his peculiar adventure, and we crept back under the wires to the crumpled little town that lived in the shadow of the Fallen city.

We went home, and lived a little longer.

My word, my beautiful shining word, was to come in very handy over the next few years. To stop time, and to be free within it, is such a power. Even now, it swells my chest to think of it. Although I can feel another pain under that one. A sharp ache of fear.

I used it when I needed time – an exam, an avoidance of reality, a morning after the night before. When I said my word, the world would freeze, and I would flit, a creature unfettered. And each time, the frozen moment drew out a little longer, giving me more. King of a silent world where I, and only I, had the liberty of freedom.

I walked between people stopped in the ignominy of their trivial lives.

I stroked the faces of pretty girls.

Kicks for those I hated. My boss. Jerry – the only moments where I seemed to be free of his shadow. Mark, who invoked in me a weak sense of pity, soured with years. My friends that were not. I am a pathetic person, I know this. And still I did it.

There were times I went to the sanctuary of the Fallen city, and let her silence wrap around me. I pretended not to search, although my gaze would sweep upward, and linger on the sides of redbrick buildings.

I never found the word again.

"You still go there, Gareth. I know you do," Mark said while we waited for Jerry at our post-work wine bar. He picked carefully at his Cajun chicken salad, and speared one scrap of flesh with the practised movement of a terminal dieter. Mark stared at me over the silver tines, the meat hovering between us. His brow was furrowed, and I did not deserve his genuine concern.

"No," I said, and rolled the word in my head. "Of course not." Jerry would bring his own penetrating questions to the conversation, I knew, and let the word slide from my head toward my waiting tongue.

I said it before Jerry joined us, and I walked off through the immobile crowd.

It took several years for me to start noticing the other effect – the slowing of time. Between the frozen moments, the seconds were stretched. A change so fractional that at first I thought it was my own imagination.

The flickers changed my mind.

They're – well, truly, I don't know what they are. Sometimes I think the flickers are time's way of trying to right itself, to catch up. Little capsules of speed, they catch me by surprise every time. One moment I'm wading through a honey-slow dribble of minutes, and the next, the world goes sharp and fast around me, and hours have passed in a handful of heartbeats. The world is slowing down, and I'm frightened. I'm frightened that I'll be trapped here when it stops, awake to the horror of being in a living body bound still as a corpse.

The jumps are few. And faster every time.

Right now, they are my window, my flash of hope.

I don't even know how long ago the last jump came. I was still at this dingy bar, I remember that, so perhaps days ago. The girl across from me is talking, her lips meet, like purple slugs, and then pull away from each other in slow-motion disgust. I flick my gaze down – as much as I am able – I'm so tired of her face, of the crust that has been sitting at the corner of her mouth now for what seems like forever.

The counter is no better. I make pictures from the scars in the wood. Use the stains to tell myself stories, but there are no new words.

I can think of only one.

I'm waiting for the jump.

If I can keep myself focused, I can use it. I can say the word. I can end this limbo. Give myself a little freedom. A lifetime of loneliness seems so small a price against this stew of waiting.

I watch where my hand sits halfway to my mouth, my fingers white against the frosted brown glass of my bottle.

And I concentrate.

Words have power. We all know it, but just how much power can one word have? That was the concept for this story. It's vaguely post-apocalyptic, suggesting that what is happening now has happened before. A boy finds a word that stops the world, and proceeds to use it to suit his own needs. And time tries to right itself.

Jack of Spades, Reversed

We must be close to New Londinium by now. The jungle is thinning and this little clearing is as good a place as any to stop and rest. My current employer sits hunched on a fallen log thick with fungi and bottle-green creeping vines. She holds her hands against her face, palms over her eyes. Her hair has turned black as feathers.

"You all right there?" I say to Louise. There's a ghost ache between my shoulder blades, as if I can feel what she's feeling.

"Shut up, Attery," she says through her fingers.

The change hurts, I remember that much and there's naught I can say that will fix her. I settle down to keep watch – there's clans out as well as the scientist-things. Chankly Bore isn't quiet, but I know all the noises it makes. The peeping tree frogs and night birds and hooting monkeys are enough to make my eyelids heavy. Leastwise there's no breaking branches, and no growling of army machines.

Louise is probably crying now – the way her shoulders are shaking – but she's one of those that keeps her sobs silent. When I met her, back when she was going mental about breathing in spore, she still had a face on her like a stone pony. Course, she was also mostly human. Thought she was above me.

I shrug off my jacket and straighten my wings. They're ragged as fuck, and they leave shiny gas-blue scales all over my fingers. Soon they'll be past healing. I flap them slow-like, and wait for the blood to pump through. Even though I know it's a dumb-fuck thing to do, I look over my shoulder at what's left of my wings. They're not looking too sweet. Shit. I flap harder.

"Stop doing that," Louise says, her hands still over her face. "I can hear you from here."

"You can't hear shit," I say, but then again it might be truth, could be already that her hearing's getting all sharp. I don't know how her change is going to go. I should try to be kinder, like keeping a death watch over a sick dog. "You feel lighter yet?" If her change goes anything like mine, her bones will turn hollow and light, easy to break.

Good for flying though.

"Shut up," she says. "I am not turning into some revolting bug."

Butterfly, I think to say, but she knows that already. She thinks she's better'n me because she comes from the Smoke and she has a ma and da and two brothers. Or had. They're all gone now. Eaten up by the war and the Chankly Bore jungle and the spore.

She's a strange one, though, even before she lost her gasmask. Wearing boy's clothing and dressed all in grey. I've never seen girls who weren't all in frocks and spangles and trying to look made-up as the Queen Vickys.

"Do you think they'll catch us?" Louise says after a while.

I shrug, even though she still has her back turned to me. "Maybe." I don't bother telling her there's worse than scientist-things all rigged up in sporesuits and carrying stun guns.

My old mates will be wandering about, looking for humans who're too far gone and putting them out of their misery – and getting fresh meat in the bargain. If ever there's a good enough reason to not sit too long – it's that. I don't fancy being no one's supper. "You ready to go on?"

"Yes." Louise tries to stand like it's nothing, but her back is all hunched and it's easy to see the way the bones are shifting. Even her face looks stretched and sharp. She takes her hands away from her eyes, and there's no hiding it now. They're black and oily and shiny. Crow eyes.

"Attery?" My name is all awkward in her mouth, and she spits out teeth.

"Yeah?" I'll wait to gather the little white pegs after she's turned around. The ivory makes good buttons.

"We're going to die, aren't we?"

Curse the Queens who go and put me in this position. I've never been one to like making a girl cry. "Do I look like a deck of cards?" I say. "I don't know your future, or even mine. I do know enough that sitting around here isn't going to do us any good."

A scream sounds out in the jungle, somewhere behind us.

"That's them," she says. "I know it is."

"So let's move, lover."

Louise is trying to get back to New Londinium, even though it's been bombed to fuck and back again. I must have been stupider than usual when I went and agreed to guide her through the jungle. Offered me a hard-boiled egg and a deck of fortune cards as payment – and well, it's been long enough since I ate an egg, and the cards will be worth something. Still makes me an idiot.

I was hoping to keep her change slow, keep her sane. It always works faster out in the wilds so I got us on one of the trains that still run. It would have taken us sweet straight to the Smoke, and no side trips into Chankly Bore. We lasted all of two stops before some fucker called us in.

Even wearing long coats and low hats, we must have been not human enough. We had to scarper and now we're miles and miles from Babylon and there're catchers after us. We're hot property. In this war, anyone who starts to change catches the attention of the scientist-things.

See, once you breathe in the spore from the old beasts you got two choices, only there's no choice at all and the one's as bad as the other.

Some people go mad; madder than, mad as, and totally fucking insane. They're the ones who have to be tied up all day and kept knocked out in case they start trying to eat themselves alive.

And then there's us. The people who start to go different, who go past madness and come out the other side, all touched by the beasts in the Space Between, and never, never the same.

We're special, at least that's what the army says. We can go back into the Space Between, and we won't get any madder. That's why the catchers want us. They want us to fly their machines back into the dark and the madness and fight the old beasts. As if that will make any difference.

"How many miles do you think we still have to go?" Louise's voice has gone flat, unhuman.

"No idea." Chankly Bore is growing faster than Dutchman's pipe, spreading out from the centre blast zone and swallowing all the cities and villages and farms. For all I know the jungle has already reached the Smoke, and ate her up just the same. We could be walking through what's left of the city.

"Fat lot of good you are," she says. "I don't know why I hired you –"

Yellow light blasts out of the greeny dark, and it cuts right across our faces and blinds me stupid.

"Stop where you are," says a man's voice, made bigger and machine-like. "We've got you surrounded."

And just how did they manage to sneak up on me on my own turf, the bastards? They had to be using shields. Hardly fair to the likes of us when the scientist-things go and use magic too. I put my hands up all slow-like. It's too late to see if my fucked-up wings will manage a flight now. They'll shoot me down. They don't need me to be able to walk or fly; all I need to be able to do is keep my finger on a trigger.

Men walk out of the shadows of vines and trunks, and only now can I hear their weird breathing and the crackle of the black plastic suits. Definitely had one of the court mages shielding them, then.

He's standing back from them, wearing leather gauntlets and a mud-slick coat. He's holding out a piece of vellum. The edges are charring under all the stress he's put it through. The vellum catches fire and he drops it to the ground, where it curls and smokes. The last of the spell ends, and all around us is a crowd of helmeted men with their beeping wands and other mechanical shit.

"Keep your hands up," says the nearest one and next to me Louise lifts her hands higher and higher and her bones crack in her back as her new wings push out of her skin.

"Attery," she says in a fast little whisper through what's left of her teeth. Her face is looking beakish, and her eyes are black. "What are they going to do to us?"

"Whatever they want." We're caught up in their stupid war against the great old beasts that come roaring through the Space Between, whether we like it or not. I hold my head up high and get a good look at the mage that sold us out. Never trust a Queen's Jack, for sure.

He takes another piece of vellum from his leather shoulder bag and folds it neat as can be, his eyes glazed away behind the plastic face mask. The vellumancy takes hold, and Louise and me are tied up magic-tighter than those poor mad buggers in Bedlam City. We can't even move a finger or a hair. The scientist-things load us into packing cases, and everything goes dark.

When the jolting stops I know that we're finally off the dirt jungle path and onto one of the old roads. They've packed me in right careful, my wings wrapped, loads of padding all about to cushion me, so it hasn't been all bad. Guess they've done much the same with Louise, and since there's naught to do but lie here and ponder how everything managed to go so wrong, I decide to sleep instead. I've never been one for trying to scrape spilled water back into a jug.

The mage opens our crates and drops the spell off us. We're in a clean white room, empty and sterile. He's the only one there, which is surprising enough.

"Don't do anything really fecking stupid." He sounds like he hasn't slept in days. Looks it too, now that the mask is gone and I can see his face, as naked and honest as a mage's can get. "I asked them if I could speak to you alone first, and it took every threat and promise I could think of to get them to agree."

I push myself out of the crate, little spongey packer-things dropping off me like the strangest snow in the world. "Seemed to work."

He shakes his head and makes a sound almost like a laugh. "Not really. Had to go and beg a favour off Vicky." He stares at me, and for all that he looks tired and drained and older than he should, his eyes are right sharp. "Know what that means?"

"You got yourself a Queen's debt to pay off." He's a Queen's Jack, with no more right to his name than a dog.

"Too true."

It means: this is important. That getting us alone is bigger even than this mage's ego and life, because he's sold himself to the Queen. I don't like that none. Don't like the implications, if you get my meaning. I turn away from the mage and help Louise out of her crate. Gives me an excuse to get a good look at just how far she's gone. Her face isn't even a little human anymore. She's a starling-headed girl with useless baby-bird wings, all bare and goosey, with just the stubs of feathers ready to grow. Her white shirt is bunched up by the new wings, and the skin I can see on her stomach and chest is still girl-soft. That's how the change is – you stay mostly human, just not human enough.

Louise tilts her head. "Bad?"

"You'll look better once the feathers grow in." And she's luckier than me, though it's not something I've told her. She'll work it out for herself, soon enough. Birds live longer than bugs, after all. "More important," I say, "This here Queen's Jack wants to have a little chat with us, all private like, before we're sent into the Space Between to go blow old beasts out of the darkness."

The Queen's Jack curls his hands up tight when I say this. He's still wearing those thick leather gauntlets. Maybe he's also less than human. "Not blow them up," he says. "Though that is what you're meant to be doing. That's what the army will think you're doing."

Mages. Never can give you a straight bloody answer. Carefully, I straighten Louise's feathers, since she's too thick to do them herself. "You'll need a proper shirt," I say to her. One that can take wings.

"We'll provide all that," says the mage. "You need to take them a message." He says it fast and soft, like he's worried that somehow, someone will be breaking the Queen's trust and recording all this.

Louise caws, and it takes me a second and a half to work out she's laughing. "A message – to the old beasts? How? Are you insane?"

And truth be told, I'm wondering if he's been at the spore himself. The old beasts are nightmare things, madness-bringers, bigger than cities, some of them. We're not exactly talking the same language, if you get me.

The mage actually grins at that, like he's got an old-fashion trick up his sleeve. "Magic," he says.

"Don't piss about."

"I'm going to put the message in your heads," he says, and I don't like the sound of that any more than you think – it's bad enough to be turned half-way into a giant butterfly and press-ganged into a war I couldn't give two shits about. I don't need a mage scrabbling about in my brainpan on top of that.

"You fucking won't," I say.

"It's really not as bad as you think. Once it's in, you won't even know it's there. It'll only activate when you're in close proximity to one of the Nar."

"Means it'll work when we get close to the old beasts," says Louise, and I'd be happy to thump her for that. Just how stupid does she think I am?

"And what do we get out of this?" Because sure as shit he's going to do this whether we say yay or nay, but I'd like to know there's at least something half-way shiny in this for me.

"If I'm right," he says. "You'll get to live."

Well, there you go then. It's shiny enough.

Ten days later my pea coat is probably in a rubbish heap somewhere, along with the rest of my mouldy old crap. The scientist-things have us kitted out in hightech. The suits are smooth as an inner tyre and body-tight, and the wing slits easy to use.

They've fed us well, and even my broken wings have been repaired with biostruts. I'm tired though. I can't sleep right. My head is full of things that shouldn't be there, and no matter what that damn mage said, my dreams are all the wrong shape and colour.

"Odd." Louise plucks at her hightech leg covers. The rubber twangs back against her thigh, and she looks up at me. The feathers have all grown in proper now, and her wings are sleek as her suit. Her buttonglass eyes don't give anything away, but she seems calm enough.

"It's just going to get weirder."

Louise clacks her beak.

There are boots in the passage. They're coming now. We're going to be strapped down in the ship they've made to travel into the Space Between.

The door opens and the scientist-things walk in. The Queen's Jack is with them, but he don't bother looking at us. His leather hands are full of vellum. We follow them out, quiet as lambs, to the Nar-space transporter.

The room is small – just big enough to hold a small gunship. They only have the one. Its hatch is open, and it looks like a trapjaw insect, black and spiky and glitter-threatening.

"You first," says a scientist-thing, and points at Louise. He hasn't bothered to learn our names. Can't right blame him.

Louise gives me a backward look. "Thanks," she says. "For trying." Her voice is flat, and maybe that's the crow talking, or maybe she just don't care anymore.

"Yeah," I say, because really, what else is there? We're fodder now. And this message isn't going to save us or no one else. Maybe I'll believe the mage knows what he's doing if Louise comes back hale and all together. Maybe.

Once she's seated, the scientist-things swarm around her, checking this and that and tightening her in place, and giving her last-minute warnings and all that shit. Louise don't nod or nothing, but I see her look once at the mage, and click her beak like she's nervous.

Then the hatch is closed, and everyone swarms out of the room, till it's just the gunship and the mage standing outside it. He's laying out his vellum in a fanned-out circle, and his mouth is moving, though I can't hear nothing from behind the big glass windows. He's careful to keep outside his circle, but there's still a chance the gate he opens could suck him through and then he's dead as dead.

He steps back, and the vellum flares. The pages stay burning, unnatural-like, and we watch and wait. I can still just make out the gunship through the fire, all hazy, like a mirage.

When the flares finally die, the gunship snaps back into focus. It's scratched and battered, smoking. The hatch opens, and inside is empty.

The mage don't look at me, just sets to laying out a new pattern with his damned papers.

"Next," says the same scientist-thing who sent Louise to her death. I feel like I just doused my head in a pail of ice water. I do what he says – it's this, or nothing. They lead me into the machine, strap me tight. The message the mage imprinted into my head is blaring peace peace peace, but I'm thinking hard over it, trying to drown it out. There's no peace for us. Not as long at the Nar are out there.

"Once you're across, we'll lose all comms, so you need to know exactly what you're doing," the scientist-thing says. It's not like he has to tell me this, Louise and me spent the last ten days simming. I could fly this fucker in my sleep. The hatch closes, and the dark glass makes it look as if I'm at the bottom of a lake. Drowning. I thumb the gun control gentle-like, wondering how they expect me to kill one of the old beasts.

The mage don't expect it at all. He said, *just drift in, just get close. You won't register as a threat if you don't start shooting.* That's how small we are.

Insignificant, Louise said, and that's a good word. A right and true one. Did Louise get in close – or was she blasted from life even though she was insignificant?

Guess I'll find out soon enough.

The room is empty now, just that mage looking at me through the dark glass, his face all twisted-like. He nods once, and then he's gone, hidden behind a wall of fire.

Everything disappears.

I'm drifting through the Space Between – Nar-space, the scientist-things call it. It's not really darkness, it's more like angles and planes that don't sit right in your brain, and colours that don't make sense, and everything warps all wrong, and so it's easier to see nothing. Nar-space feels like the jelly inside an eyeball, like drowning in diesel and rainbows.

I shut down the engines, take my thumb off the firing button. The little gunship spins about, leaf-lazy. I don't even know if there are any old beasts out in this part of madness. I could just be flying around forever, until I come back all mummified.

The gunship hits something, and bounces off. I spin upside down, and thank Vicky and all her minions I'm strapped in tighter than a moth in a spider's web.

A silver light, thin as a fishing line, cuts through the dark. It comes to me and wraps around the nose of my gunship. I'm frozen. Damn the mage and all his stupid ideas, I should just start shooting and try to take at least one with me when I go. My thumb squeezes down, just the smallest bit. The peace peace peace is bugling inside my head and I squeeze harder but my body don't listen.

Fine, I think, and take my hand off the trigger. If I'm going to go to my death, it may as well be a choice *I* make, and not one some fucker in a court or a laboratory made for me. I unclip all the buckles, and let myself go.

"Come on, then," I yell to the madness. "She's dead. I'm as good as. Come on and do it clean, cleaner than those bastards back in the real world."

I'm tired of scientist-things and mages using me for their god-damned war and not even having the decency to ask me my bloody name first.

"I'm Attery St John, you fuckers." I bow to the shapes in the darkness. "A pleasure to make your acquaintance."

More silver lines come for me, wrapping my gunship up like a silkworm.

A panel of dark glass cracks and one of the fishing line things is inside, nosing about, blind as can be. I can't close my eyes. Not since I changed, and all I can do is float here, and let the old beast eat me.

It prods at my face, and the touch of it is a trigger. The thing the mage stuck in my head breaks open and the hatch fills with magic. The tendril pulls back, puffing a cloud of spore. The spore and magic meet, and I can feel them both tearing through my brain, mixing up.

They're talking.

They're honest to Queens fucking talking.

They talk for longer than years, and just seconds, and then the tendrils turn to me and hold my face, gentle. They're tapping at me, all playful, and the air is full of spore and I'm choking on it but it's sweet and good and I can see the past and present and future and everything.

~stay?~ they say inside my head. ~pretty here. safe~

And I think, well, why the fuck not. And the hatch opens and I'm in the Space Between, but I'm all right-like, and the silver fishing lines have me, and then I'm inside –

Oh, inside the old beasts and there is Louise, bright and shiny black, her beak open in a bird smile.

She's real as real, and I wasn't expecting the feeling that runs through me now, a human thing – relief. All around us, the Nar touch and talk, explain the world in new dimensions, taking away our deaths and giving us a new kind of sanity, one that even Queen Vicky with her court mages wouldn't understand.

I drift up to Louise, my wings spreading, growing bigger and bluer and that's okay because right here right now, that's as it should be.

There's nothing strange about being a boy who is also a butterfly, or being a starling who is also a girl.

~yes~ say the old beasts in the tones of parents who have been trying to explain simple things to small children.

"I could have pressed the trigger," I say to Louise.

"He didn't think you would."

Never trust a mage. Not even the ones on your side. I smile. I wonder if the scientist-things know what it was he did right under their noses. If the Queen knows what her debt really bought her. How many more of the changelings will he send through before Queen Vicky cottons on and hangs him as a traitor, I wonder.

It doesn't matter.

There are others already here. We were not the first.

We won't be the last.

We are in the beasts now, and we are them and they are us and one day there will be a new world, and we will go back, and New Londinium will be the jungles and the Space Between and Bedlam and Babylon and we will all have changed.

And perhaps, like gods, we will raise the dead.

The Jack of Spades, Reversed

This is one of the shorts based on another work – in this case an unfinished novel that I went into with the vague idea of an Arthurian Return story in the style of Edward Lear meets Lovecraft. As my works tend to do, it mutated into something else. The basic idea is that perhaps the monsters are trying to save us in their own peculiar way. And that not all King Arthurs are what we expect (or want).

MOTHER, CRONE, MAIDEN

"Seeing into the future is not a straight line," my mother says. "You are given the choice of a hundred paths through a treacherous swamp. Some will lead you safely onwards, others drown you, and sometimes it's hard to tell which is which."

I'm sitting at a polished wooden desk in our family library, surrounded by the dusty rustling of knowledge. My mother has been explaining these dry facts at me for the entire afternoon. I press the point of my quill into the wood and watch the split climb up the shaft.

House Malker has always been noted for its excess of Saints, and our lives are dictated by omens and Visions. We are ruled by our reliance on the drug scriv, the gateway to our power. Scriv: more precious than any metal or jewel or life. Without it, we are nothing. There is never enough, and there is certainly never enough to waste more than a few grains on the future of a girl.

Were I a boy, my father would have overseen my education and had me tutored by the best of the university's learned men. Instead, I am being taught how to tell the future by my mother.

She's still talking, her voice as distant and meaningless as the screeching of the sea mews over the cliffs near our mansion. "For an important business or political decision, it has not been unheard of for a Saint to try for the same Vision ten or fifteen times. A Saint can also choose the manner in which they see." She taps three pieces of coloured glass on the desk, selects one. With the red glass in her hand she says, "Pay attention, Ilven."

"I am." This is not exactly true. Through the narrow windows I can see Felicita on the far edge of our property, waving at the house from our spinney. Our meeting place. Her House is greater than mine, and so Mother encourages this friendship, even as she catalogues all Felicita's flaws.

"Perhaps if you looked in my direction instead?" My mother sidles toward a painting of a battle between the Lammers and our age-old enemies, the Mekekana, and holds up the red glass. "This is emotion," she says, and the picture shows me only the brightest and most blazing things. The blood of the dead is washed away. She swaps the glass for the blue. "Political decisions." The picture reveals now not the glory of the war, but the cold black blood that fuelled it. The Mekekana's vast beetle-ships become savage, their barbaric machines cold and iron-dark as they crawl on their immense wheels, crushing our bones beneath them.

Despite my desire to leave this room and its towers of oppressive books, I find myself interested. No one has ever explained the way Saints make decisions to me, as if somehow I was always too stupid and small to understand. They have merely taught me by rote, and expected that to be enough. "And the green?"

"We'll call this personal power," she says. Again the focus shifts; what appeared important before becomes subdued.

All futures are tinted by the way in which you choose to view them.

Here then is a truth only Saints understand: Knowing the future is not about knowing the future. It's about which choice to make.

That is why you can never get a straight answer from a Saint, for they have none to give.

I am sixteen and to be married in a matter of weeks. I had no say in this future. My father chose him for me and I have never seen the man's face, nor will I until I am presented to him on my wedding day. He lives many miles upriver, on a wine estate. I'm told the wine he makes is very fine. I wonder how many paths my father bothered to look down before he made up his mind.

My mother was unhappy with the decision, measuring out scriv with a tiny silver spoon and trying for different ways to see her Vision. Eventually she gave up and tried with cards instead, and all Saints know that cards are useless for anything more than parlour games. Even this failed her, and so she has accepted my father's choice.

I do not accept it. Not when I have something I want more.

My first kiss was at fourteen, in one of the many dark and draughty rooms of Felicita's home. I don't know why her brother did it, perhaps because he himself was off to be married and I seemed like a safe thing to use to still his own fears. Owen was already a man, and I think it was the only time he ever paid me the slightest attention. He was high on scriv and I could taste his futures on his tongue. I was in one of them, slight and faint.

After that he left and life carried on much the same. I see Owen only very occasionally, and always I am studiously ignored. I watch his wife for weaknesses, for ill health. She seems immune to my wishes.

I have never told Felicita about this kiss. Sometimes at night when I can't sleep, I let myself remember the way he came to me, the way he tipped my head back. The same memory over and over in rhythm with the waves. The ocean becomes the salt taste of his mouth, and I wish that there were a future where my House and House Pelim tied themselves together and I had Owen. Perhaps it is not too late for me.

Who knows what course I could still take to bring about the future of my desire? I do not expect much – one man. It will not change the world, not to ask for something so small.

It is a week until my wedding. The gold silk has been fitted, the feasts have been planned, and we will travel upriver in a matter of days. My parents and brother will be the only ones returning. Mother has become waspish as the day draws closer. She has discovered herself burdened with an autumn pregnancy, a prospect I find humiliating, although my father is pleased. He expects another son.

It's this good humour of his and the bustle of the household that allow me the opportunity to steal a thimbleful of scriv from his guarded stores. Even if he discovers my theft, my wedding is too soon for him to want to spoil my skin with bruises.

I lock my room, set out my scriv silver, and divide the dust into three fat lines. Next to it on the desk is a letter from Felicita, passed to me by my most trusted servant. Felicita wants us to run to Old Town tomorrow, for just one day, and pretend we are not tied to the rules of our Houses. We could spend the hours clinging to our illusion of freedom, and buy trinkets from market stalls run by Hobs, visit the low tea shops where the poets and artists gather. Perhaps even see one of the street operas that I have heard the servants talk of. It's appealing – the idea of this last little burst of free will. I need to send her an answer soon.

First, and more important, I would see myself a new future. The smell of bitter citrus coils up from the scriv as I lower my little glass tube and inhale sharply. The burst of orange behind my eyes is followed by a faint acrid taste at the back of my throat. I swallow, close my eyes, and wait for my Vision to take hold.

The blackness swirls. After a few moments it greys, and I am pitched into a new body. Or rather, a familiar body weighted by time and children. It is Longest Day, our slow and lazy celebration of midsummer. My husband has brought us down to Pelimburg for the festivities, and we are at a garden party hosted by House Canroth. Felicita stands opposite me, her thick auburn hair pulled back and tamed, her hands locked over the small swell of her stomach. She is still in that stage where pregnancy is not yet a trial of endurance.

"They're very handsome," she says, and smiles at my two sons. "They grow so fast, every time I see them I can't quite believe how tall they are."

My daughter, mouse-like and clingy, hides in my skirts, unwilling to approach this woman she last met as a babe-in-arms. "And yours." Although this is not quite true. The oldest at least has some of her features, but the moon-faced younger boy is not quite as fortunate.

"Oh, come here." Felicita steps forward to grab at my hands. "Must you be so formal? I've missed you." She kisses both my cheeks and curls her fingers in mine. We cling together like this, our hands hidden in the folds of our dresses. "I miss you, Ilven," she says again, soft as the brush of rabbit-tail grass against my skin. Guilt and misery taste like bile. I want so much to miss her as much as she does me. And I almost do. There is one I miss more, the man I dream of when I am with my red-faced husband, the one my sons should have looked like.

Even as I hold Felicita, I look over her shoulder for his face. As the head of House Pelim, he might have been too busy to accept the invitation.

No. There he is: Pelim Owen, pale-skinned with his dark auburn hair. He seems to stand taller than anyone else here, and magic and power swirl around him so thickly, a cloak of air and fire. I am the only one who can see him as he truly is. He is dressed in riding black and already bored by the frivolity around him. His meek and pretty wife and daughters are nowhere to be seen, and a moment of giddy happiness rises in me. Then he turns and smiles, and holds out his hand, and his wife steps from the crowd, takes it, and smiles back.

"We should visit more often," I say to Felicita.

"I'd like that." We squeeze each other's fingers tighter.

I pull back out of the Vision. This is my safe and open path, perhaps even the one my father saw for me when he decided my marriage. I am prosperous, healthy, I have produced children, and have held on to my ties of friendship with House Pelim. It is all that has ever been expected of me.

Outside my window a bird is singing liquidly. One of the blue-faced mynahs has come down from the high forests above our property. If it stays too long near the cliffs, the sea mews will mob it; peck it to death unless it escapes. A sign, if I wish to take it. The mynahs can be tamed and taught to say a few words if you are patient enough. This is what I will be, a tamed and talking bird, out of my element.

Taking this much scriv is not something I've done before. I sip at a cup of cold tea to pace myself. There are tales passed down by Saints about the damage we can do to our bodies. My maternal grandfather went to his grave early, spitting up pieces of his lungs on his way. I have no memory of this – he died before I was born – but I have heard my mother recount the tale and my stomach clenches. Is this fear? Or perhaps I am already doing some irreversible harm? I banish these worries. They are unimportant when I have so great a goal in mind. With my tea finished, I lean forward to try for a second Vision.

I slip into this one faster, a headlong tumble. I am now, or so close to now it hardly matters. I am running through Pelimburg at night, dressed in simple clothes, with a small hiking bag over my shoulders. I have covered my hair and rubbed dirt into my skin. Even so I am too blond and pale for this city. Monstrous people watch me as I run past. I am lost in the alleyways and warrens of Old Town. If I go back, I will be worse than one of the magicless children that some Houses breed. The men of my family will not take well to my disobedience. My fingers cling tight to the straps of my hiking bag. We do not talk of the women who have dishonoured their families. People do not say their names.

But what worse fate waits for me – did I think to run to Owen's apartments and throw myself at his feet? He will laugh at me, turn me over to my parents, and never look at me again.

I will cease to exist.

"Kss, kss," hisses a man's voice, calling my attention. I glance back. One of the lower-caste Hobs is watching me with sly interest. He pushes himself away from the wall he's leaning on and ambles toward me. My heart slams faster, and I push my way through the crowded streets. He seems to always be just behind me, hunting me through Pelimburg's narrow arteries. My feet slip on the cobbles and I trip, smashing my cheek against the edge of the stone sidewalk, bruising my hands and knees. He is almost upon me. I scrabble up, and look this way and that, searching for a place to slip away. I duck into a black-mouthed alley thick with stacked crates and piles of rotting litter.

For a moment, I am safe, and then I hear the smack of bare feet on the wet cobbles. I duck behind a perilous tower of rain-swollen crates, and wait, holding my breath until my chest burns.

"It went in here." A high-pitched voice. Not my pursuer then. I sigh in relief, and stand. A circle of dark-skinned Hoblings pens me in the alleyway, their skip ropes slapping against the cobbles. They have folded them over like nooses.

"Get away," I say to them, trying to keep my calm. They are, after all, just children.

The closest one grins and lashes out with the end of her rope. A small boy behind her shrieks in laughter. I press my back against the stone walls and dig my fingernails into crumbling moss. If I scream, will the sharif come running to my rescue?

I do not want to face the Hobs, I want to be saved from my own stupidity. What girl runs from her wedding and dares to bring such humiliation down on her family name? I do not know what idiocy made me slip off the wherry taking us to Samar and trudge back along the riverbanks.

"Here," says a sharif in a white uniform, and the Hoblings scatter like cats. "Little bastards," he yells at them, before he turns to me. "And what's this then? You've fallen from your glass tower?" He snorts.

"I'm – visiting family," I say. "I got lost." And now I wish I had thought of some cover story before I had a run-in with the sharif. No House daughter would walk in Pelimburg's streets without an escort at the very least.

"Are you now – then you'd best follow me."

I do not move.

"Come on, then. Little lost thing." He laughs. "I daresay someone will be along to collect their missing property soon enough." The sharif folds his hand over my wrist and drags me from the alleyway. My bones contract and grow brittle, my body folds in on itself, withered and wrinkled. The sharif has pulled me many decades into the future, to a Longest Night celebration.

It is bitter, this cold, it works its way into my bones and freezes my joints stiff. I don't often go out of my youngest brother's house but his children insisted, and they still have a laughing interest in this old-maid aunt of theirs. They are shrieking in their excitement, dashing between the legs in the crowd. In my day, behaviour like this would never have been tolerated; my brother has been lax with the nannies. I would speak to him about it but I already know he will not listen to a thing I say.

We're all gathering at the centre square that usually hosts the market. Under the vast tree that once used to shade the slave pens where the bats were kept, the Longest Night drummer is waiting to bring in the new year. This is supposed to be the night of change where for one starlit moment everyone in every city and village is equal, princes and beggars alike.

Longest Night has always been given over to secret meetings, where men and women, Lammers and Hobs, lie with whomever they like. It is a moment without consequences. Perhaps now that he is over the mourning period of his wife's death, Owen will be here along with all the other Great Houses. I lose myself in the throng of merrymakers, stepping aside to let the puppeteers and fire-spinners rush past me, always, always looking for his face.

He is old now. Grim, his eyes heavy, but he still has the Pelim good looks, the handsome sneer and the sharp cheekbones. Even the gray at his temples is distinguished.

"Owen," I say. It is allowed, this informality. The taste of his name is warmed honey, spiced with lemon and cloves.

He stops and squints at me. I can see from his frown that he does not really know who I am. I push my silver hair back and raise my face to him, pretend that I am a girl caught in a dark room, still beautiful and willow-thin. "Ilven," I say. "It's Ilven." He cannot have forgotten that moment, the way he held my waist and tilted my mouth to his. He merely needs reminding.

"Ah." He looks around at the crowd. "The spinster." His hard mouth twists.

Sour nausea rises in my throat. I had thought that the years would have smothered the shame of running from my wedding. I falter for something to say to keep him with me. "It's a pleasure to see you again." The words are too desperate and too inane at the same time. We have nothing to say to each other. I barely know him, and he knows me not at all.

Fireworks burst distantly over the faraway cliff houses. His face is thrown into blue and green and red, and I see him as through shards of coloured glass. His hands are hidden from me, tucked deep into the pockets of his winter coat. "Likewise," he says, but he is still not looking at me, just through me, past me, over me.

"I was sorry to hear of your loss."

This snaps his attention to my face, and his dark eyes clear. "You're here alone?"

"With my brother's family." I step closer to him, so that the heat from his body can warm my cold heart. He is free for me to have now, a widower and an old man. Surely it is in my power to finally win him?

"They will be looking for you," he says, and turns. "Perhaps you should go back to them." And he walks away and I lose him in the fires and screams.

Gris! I force myself out of the Vision. The sound of my panting breaths echoes in my room, filling it up with my distress.

Not this one, not this one. A path like this will bring me nothing I want. I do not need the auguries of birds to confirm it. There has to be a better path I can walk down. Shivers rattle me, and perspiration gathers at the nape of my neck. It could be shock or the start of a scriv fever. I do not care. The final line of scriv is still waiting and I want it – want it to show me something different. My tea is finished. My fingers crawl to the thin glass pipe, tap at it. Too soon.

Instead, I drag my hand away and pluck a strand of hair from my head. The slight sting helps me focus. I wrap the strand around one index finger, digging it into the flesh so that the tip of my finger purples and begins to ache. I wait until it is numb and white before unwinding the strand again. Pins and needles spark down my finger, a delicious pain that keeps me from thinking of my final Vision.

The fine hair has left small ridges in my finger. It is with a morbid fascination I watch my flesh slowly return to its proper shape. If only we could do that with our hearts, deform them to our whims and pleasure, secure in the knowledge that they will always return to a perfect state, as if they had never been hurt at all.

The shivers are growing worse now and the silk of my dress has glued itself to my back. My mother will not be amused if I fall ill so soon before we leave. She will take it as a personal insult. The room tilts and I cling to the desk, waiting for the dizziness to pass.

The clock sounds loud in the silence, tiny hammers tapping against my temple with mechanical precision. Enough time has passed. I snort my final line of scriv and let it pull me underwater.

I rise, gasping, ocean water streaming down my hair. I wipe the salt sting from my eyes and look around me. The sand is strange under my feet, as if I'm barely touching it.

"Took you long enough," says the boy standing before me. He is brown and short, no older really than I am now. His hair is dark and curling, his slanted eyes grey and green. A Hob. And why would I come at the summons of a Hob, of all things? No servant would presume such a thing of me.

"Where am I?" The beach is an unfamiliar one, rocky and wild, and the black-backed gulls are screaming at us. I have always hated that sound and my heart is stuttering. The seawater feels sticky, like the sweat of a fever.

He shrugs. "Lambs' Island."

The waves rush around my feet, dragging insistently at the sand under my heels, trying to pull me back. Lambs' Island is a forbidden place, full of ghosts and old Mekekana iron. I am hollow inside, hungry. I have no memory of how I got here. Did I drown or was I rescued by this Hob with his insolent face and his parody of House fashion? The question then: Do I owe him anything?

"You have something I want," he says and holds out his hand.

"I do?"

"A gift, for Pelim Owen."

In the old stories, the ones I read as a child and would now never confess to knowing, lovers pass trinkets to one another – little things they hand over to show their secret passions. Is this what I have done here? Started an affair with my beautiful Owen, passing gifts between us via this Hob? I look down and realise I am naked. I have nothing to give. I can see the sand through my feet, just faintly.

"The hairpin will do," he says.

I touch my hair with one hand, find the silver and jewelled stick still tangled there with little strands of red seaweed. A crab as small as a pea is nestled against one of the silver-green leaves. I flick it off and hand my hairpin over. It is a good choice, a symbol of my House. I am handing myself to Owen, marking him.

The Hob reaches out to take it and as he does a terrible hunger rises through the core of my body. I can almost smell the blood and meat of him over the salt and dune brush. I shake my head, and focus on a memory of flying. Of falling, arms outstretched.

The Hob slips my hairpin into his waistcoat pocket. "Here." He holds out an empty palm, waiting for me.

"And?"

"Payment, freely given."

I do not understand what it is that compels me to touch the cup of his hand. The Hob's pulse thrums under my fingers. His life force flows through me, warming the sluggish blood in my veins.

He snatches his hand back with a rueful grin. "Not everything, not now. I still have things to do." He looks at the small silver mark I have left on his skin. "You can have the rest later, boggert. Give me a few days yet."

"The pin – you'll take it to Owen?" Why can I not remember anything of earlier meetings with this lover of mine, surely his ocean kisses would have stained my skin? The word boggert swims lazily in my mind, rippling eel-like. Am I dead, then? Is this how I will make Owen mine?

"Oh if there's one thing I can promise you, it's that."

"Has he sent me any message?" I cling to the moment that will come, of lovers meeting. To life, even as this Hob uses me. I have never been a fool. This thing I have done is sure to bring death out of the sea. What does it matter now if I play this Hob's game? We will both have the man we want. Our reasons are different, but the ending will be the same. I find I don't care.

"A message, no, I –" He frowns, then slips into a smile. "You want me to take him one?"

"Will you tell him..." Already I am imagining Owen's body against me, our arms and legs tangled ribbons of kelp. I see a world where the ocean is turned red and the fires burn Pelimburg to the ground and the smoke hangs over the city in funerary black. I see a world where Pelim Owen is brought to me by storms unimaginable, and it is my hand he reaches out for. So this is how I win my lover's heart – through death and treachery. "Will you tell him I miss him?"

"I can do that."

The water is tugging me back, but it does not matter. Owen is mine. Soon, so soon we will be together. The waters close cold over my head and my earlier sorrows are washed away.

I rise gasping, the taste of scriv burning my sinuses and throat. I choke, and rub streaming salt tears from my eyes. This one. All it will take from me is one small sacrifice. It will have to be carefully arranged. I pull a sheet of paper from my stationery drawer and send Felicita an answer to her earlier message, setting a time to meet at our spinney.

When I go to sleep, I am more contented than I have been in months, or even in years. The calm of my decision lulls me, brushes ill dreams from my brow.

In the morning I watch Felicita from my window. The drizzle adds to her impatience and after a few stretched minutes, she turns and walks away, taking the rocky path down to the road. In a half hour I will be safe, assured that she is well on her way to Old Town and the Levelling Bridge.

No one stops me from leaving the house and crossing the goat-cropped lawns toward Pelim's Leap. It is as if I have become a ghost already. Only when I go right to the very edge of the cliffs do I hear them shouting from far away. The wind and stinging rain buffets me to the last crumbling stones and pulls my hair free. The white-blond strands dance and tangle in front of my face, but the little hairpin is still secure. It feels overly heavy, bending my head down and pushing me toward the seething grey waters far below.

Here is the last truth of Saints: We will always choose the path which brings us the most power.

I spread my arms, and let the wind tip me.

A prequel story to my novel When the Sea is Rising Red, *it's from the point-of-view of a minor character whose actions are the catalyst that sets the entire story in motion. It's about being able to tell the future, but not necessarily being able to make the right choices. If there even are right ones to be made.*

This Reflection of Me

I live in a bone house.

The last room – that's mine. You can tell because the brass handle is still shiny, polished by my master's palms. At night I walk down passageways tarry with decay, with the years' grime. I pass the other doors. Their silent wooden faces.

All rooms in my house are quiet.

The master is away in his black-rigged ship, held aloft with hands grey and green in the dawn. In my mind, I see the waves' fingers turn white as they clutch at the decks, perhaps pulling a man overboard.

I close the dream, and step out into the hallway. The floor is old, the boards worn thin at the edges, not meeting. If you drop something small, it will be lost to the people that live beneath.

The others up here are all dead. Seven girls brought to me, their dowries gather dust next to their bones.

Sometimes, I go to look upon them, to glean what I can from their faces, from the way their screams have solidified in the dusty flesh. The door to their burial room is never locked, for he knows how I like to sit in their silence. I'm happiest when it is quiet, when I can lean into them, nestle close, and hear only the muted call of nightjars or owls. I curl up to my favourite, lean into the length of her body, and pull her arms carefully around me. Ivory clacks, and dust falls. I must move with painstaking sloth, for fear I break this delicate embrace. Ah, love is such a brittle thing.

Outside, far below me, the streets are quiet. No one walks along the cobbles. Only the wind comes salt-laden to the window, and whispers in my ears. I nod, and leave my plaything, my sweet girl, to go and see out the narrow window. Grime has shuttered the glass, and it takes all my thin-armed strength to push the window free. I lean over the ledge, gazing down to the distant water.

Moonlight silvers the city, edging her spires and turrets with halos. The sea speaks again, the wind carrying her message to me. And there! I see the sails in the harbour, silhouettes against the streaked horizon.

The master is home.

"She's a pretty one," he says. He knows I saw him bring her in. I always watch.

I see her only briefly, shining under her cloud of dark hair. The others were so pale, so gentle, I could not help but be drawn to their cleanness; the soft golden edges of them. I do not answer him; instead I look in the mirror, and comb out my hair with the new ivory-handled brush he has brought me. I like this gift better than the other. Under the moonlight, my hair shines with a black so rich that it seems almost blue.

The girl is an intrusion. She breaks the quiet with her childish noise, flittering as she does from room to room, like a black dove trapped in a locked house. All thundering heart beat and the clatterclap of wings.

At night, when he should be with me, my master ruts in her bed, his pale arse like flyblown fruit between the dusk of her thighs. I stop watching through the rotted boards. The ivory handle breaks when I fling my brush across the room and into the scowling face I see reflected at me from the unmarked mirror. The swarthy face glares back and then she is gone. I press my ear to the boards.

"What sound was that?" Her voice is high and cool.

"Ah, nothing, nothing, my sweet. A bat maybe, or the baker's cat running from roof to roof."

"If there are rats in the attic, my love, I'll instruct the servants to set traps."

"Not rats, my sweet. I told you it was but the baker's cat. We'll hear no more sounds, see?"

I listen from the walls, from the cracks. The dove coos, trying to keep him to her bed.

"Must you go?"

"If you like the finery I bring you, then I must," he says. "No seas give up their treasures without a fight."

"You said you were a merchant."

"And so I am."

My black prince merchant, with his ship of darkness, has set sail once more. He's left her alone in the house, the servants instructed to obey her.

The first night he is gone, I see her rummaging through my master's things, her fingers quick as darting fish. She reminds me of a dove no longer – the frantic wings have given way to furtive glances. She is a ship's rat, scratching through treasure.

"Do you have the key for the attic?"

The servant shakes her head, mute with fear. All these are loyal to me, they will not speak to her.

She has found it while I sleep. My master's key.

I hear the tread of her slippered feet on the stairs that lead to my house of bones, and I am instantly awake, curled and ready as a cat.

The key slides into the oiled lock; just the faintest snick of sound, the barest tumble of gears, and the door is opened. She carries a candle, or perhaps an oil lamp. The light spreads disease into my muffled gloom, infecting with its flicker.

The shadows pull around me, cloaking me with their soft quick fingers, and I pad after her as she makes her way with halting steps down the passage of my home.

Tonight her arms are too stiff for love. I lay the girl down, ease off the embroidered slippers my master gave her, unbutton her chemise. I stretch out against her, pressing my chest against the soft swell of her, against the ripeness of her body, before I pull a silken blanket over us and fall asleep with my breath fluttering her lashes.

Light comes stealing into my house. Even the morning bird-song cannot break my mood. Looking down at the girl's face, so peaceful in repose, I can see now the beauty that my master saw. She is prettier than all the others, this reflection of me.

My very first pro sale, so it holds a special place for me. Already the repeating motifs of my work are there, germinating: the ocean in the background, the retellings (in this case, Bluebeard), and the ending that leaves you uncertain as to who is the good and who the evil. Grey is much more interesting.

Counter Curse

There are always three stories. The winner tells one, the loser tells another, and the third, the one we could call truth if we looked at it sidelong through a piece of shattered glass, that is the story that fades soonest, forgotten even as it tells itself.

There is no room for truth in love.

Here is the story that eats its own tail. We must tell it quickly in dreams and whispers, before there is nothing left of it but an eye that watches and a mouth too choked to speak. It starts in the forest, where all the wild things learn their sleights and magics, in a castle, where all the tame things learn their place.

The king and queen are not important to this story (they have their own – it is short and bloody and sad, and it ends before it should), instead, there is a man who works with the castle beasts, with the horses and the falcons and the ravens. He was not born in the castle, but he grew up in the forest that surrounds it, and he has a talent for speaking the tongues of animals. He is well-paid. He has a wife who is clever and almost beautiful when the candles are low. He is a comfortable man, with a comfortable life. He enjoys his work, he loves his wife. He loves his daughter.

When she was born, he likes to say, all the animals from the castle came to pay their respects. Every beast from the stable and keep, mouse and war horse both. It might even be true. Freya is smart like her mother, and she has her father's talent, although it takes a different form. This doesn't bother her. She plays with her magic like a princess plays with a golden ball – it is precious, and yet, it is just a toy. She makes rushes dance across the castle flagstones, teaches hares to stay away from the castle gardens, sets the great candles of the watchclocks to burn bright and high, their flames charmed into a flickering puppetry.

She is a plain girl, though there are no mirrors to tell her this, and it does not matter for her suitors are many and varied in temperament. She finds them amusing. Freya is waiting for love to come to her on bright and shining hooves, to be a roaring thing that takes her completely by surprise – the way she sees it still for her parents, who hold hands when they walk at night, and who laugh over spilled milk and bruised fruit. They have learned to cut the sour parts out of their lives and enjoy what they have left.

Instead, her mother brings home a girl so beautiful that it blinds her.

"This is Inga," says her mother, as she pushes the girl forward. Her hair is a flow of sunlight against the kind of milky skin that terrible poets seem to favour in their verse. Her eyes are deep and black and wide as forest pools. She smells like pine needles. She smells like winter. She smells like magic.

Inga mutters her hello, awkward and out of place. She has some tragic story – a family dead – these things happen. She was working as a maid. Freya's mother – whose needlework is small and fine as though it were stitched by mice (and perhaps it is) – found her barefoot and ash-painted in the lower kitchens, scrubbing out the blackened pots. The lowest job for the lowest scullery maid.

"I could taste her magic," she says to Freya's father. "How anyone could not have noticed..."

It's true. She has that same strange under-the-tongue taste of air that is too cold which Freya and her father both have. In Inga, it is sharper than splinters, sweeter than sugar shards. Even so, Freya knows that she is stronger still, that Inga's real power lies in her beauty.

"Welcome, sister," Freya says, and when Inga looks up at her with those drowning eyes, Freya knows nothing will ever be true again.

It doesn't take long for the beautiful to see the beautiful; after all, they have eyes only for their own reflections. The son of the king and queen is one of those pretty fools who are not malicious so much as bred only to believe the lies they are fed. He is only as vain and shallow as he has been brought up to be. This is what Freya tells herself when the prince begins to send Inga gifts of delicate necklaces and embroidered slippers.

She watches Inga fall in love with the idea of her prince.

"You shouldn't," she tells her one day. They are both sitting at the kitchen table, peeling potatoes and carrots with slender sickle-bladed knives. Or at least, Freya is. Inga is daydreaming, her head pillowed on one palm as she watches Freya's knife swoop lazily through the air, slicing gentle skirts of orange away from her dancing carrot.

"Shouldn't what?" Her eyes are half-lidded, her voice slow as a waking dream.

The carrot and knife dance faster, the blade paring away at its partner. Freya waits for the tremble in her throat to die. When she is sure she will speak without betraying herself, she says, "Don't trust the sons of kings. They don't marry the foster daughters of court magicians. They marry princesses. You would be nothing more than a- than a dalliance. There are others who would give you more."

Inga turns her head like a hunting snake and stares at her. "You're jealous."

And Inga is right but for all the wrong reasons. "Not – not – not of you," Freya tries to say but the words are all caught up in her throat and crawling over each other like maggots in meat, and besides, Inga is already on her feet, her dark eyes like blown-out stars, her hair swirling in the gale of her anger. She storms from the kitchen and slams the door behind her.

On the table, Freya's carrot has been pared down to the pale core, lying in a bed of orange curls like flayed skin. She gathers the remains and chops them dully to add to the evening meal.

The prince can be charming, can be witty, can be attentive. These are the things that make him as popular as he is among the court ladies, Freya knows. Where before he was never someone she paid overly much attention to, now Freya finds herself waiting in the places she knows he frequents, learning his times and routines that she can follow him without following him. She wants to be able to know her enemy, her rival, to know him so completely that any move he makes she will be assured hers is better. When the prince sends Inga a set of earrings made of silver and sapphire, Freya carves a small and beautiful box with an intricate locking mechanism for her to keep them in. "If you wear them, you might lose them," she tells her foster sister, and reluctantly, the earrings are hidden away. Inga keeps the box by her bed, and soon forgets to open it.

Freya does the same for each thing he sends to Inga – finds some way of reducing it, hiding it, replacing it with a gift more practical. She dresses Inga in gloves she has knitted, tunics she has edged with tiny embroidered wrens, shoes she has lined with rabbit fur. Each time she sees Inga wearing one of these, she is certain that she has stitched her foster sister closer to her.

Inga wears her gifts with the careless ignorance of the beautiful. At night she begs Freya's help and Freya shreds her dreams and weaves silk dresses out of spiders' webs and dancing slippers from the sparkle of starlight on ice. She twists straw into golden bangles and thistles into jewelled hair combs. She dresses her foster sister in her magic.

When the magician and his wife are asleep, Inga crawls through the window to join the prince at his innumerable balls and dances. Each time she kisses Freya's cheeks fiercely and makes her promise to say nothing.

Always, Freya promises, and keeps the memory of the kisses burned into her skin.

She is losing Inga, though she knows that the truth is she never had her.

The problem with broken hearts is that they are sharp and jagged and filled with long fine shards. Broken hearts are cruel. Broken hearts can see only their own misery.

Because she wasn't the one Inga fell in love with, Freya feeds her jealousy at attentively as a watchman feeding twigs to a fire. As Inga has grown more beautiful, so Freya has grown more powerful. She has found how easy it is to shed her skin and sprout feathers. She turns into a white raven and soars over the forests when the prince goes hunting. He is always so quick to kill, like an animal, she thinks. Like a beast. She can no longer see him as human, he is a hunting thing and all he touches he destroys.

The prince is obsessed with a white hart that lives in the forest, and he chases the deer through spring and summer and autumn and winter, seeing no other prey as worthy. When he finally brings it down and stains the white snow crimson, Freya is there to see it. She lands, raven-skinned, on the corpse, and the prince's men laugh and say it is a sign – a white raven to mark the death of the white stag.

"A ten-point stag," says one of the men. "An excellent shot, sire." He looks to Freya. "The bird's wings would make a pretty ornament."

The prince smiles and shakes his head. "I have what I want," he says as Freya lurches skywards.

Later, the stag's pale head is mounted in the castle hall. It looks down over the courtiers, over the lords and ladies. It is a reminder to Freya that the prince is a beast who collects trophies. That he cares only for the chase and the kill.

It might not be the truth, but it is Freya's truth.

Her heart festers, her hate and jealousy cushioning it in her breast. And like a sickening thing, her mind is poisoned, and at night she dreams of beasts and teeth, of murders and betrayals.

It is Inga's seventeenth birthday, and the prince has sent her a gown trimmed in ermine, a golden circlet for her brow. The court-ladies have long since given up – against the shimmer of Inga's beauty they cannot compare. Like the mystical white hart he once chased through the frozen forest, the Prince has found something beautiful that he must have, he hunts Inga as completely as she hunts him.

They deserve each other, Freya thinks, and weaves the gift she has designed for her foster sister.

"He loves you," she says that evening, as she helps Inga tie the laces of her tunic and dress, as she straightens the hair combs that hold her golden mane in place. *He loves you like a white stag, like a trophy for his hall.*

"He does," Inga smiles, it is dreamy, soft and Freya hates it. It makes her look like an imbecile. They deserve each other.

"What if he strays?" she asks.

Inga frowns. "That would never happen –"

"Real life isn't a children's tale," Freya says. Her fingers twist and braid, twist and braid, twist and braid. "Look at his father – the old queen must watch and pretend she sees nothing when he takes court ladies as lovers. Younger, prettier women who replace her. One day that might also happen-"

"Shut up!" Inga says fiercely. "He's not like that."

"Or you," Freya continues as though she has not heard. "Your head might be turned by the wink of a nobleman or knight. After all, you wouldn't be the first queen to run off with her husband's most trusted companion."

"I hate you," Inga whispers, her eyes glassy. "You've always been jealous that the prince saw me and not you."

"Not true," Freya says. "But I can make it so these things never happen." It's a lie, of course. There is no magic that will make someone fall in love any more than curses can make them fall out of love. But Inga doesn't know this. Her magic is weaker than Freya's and she doesn't have her sister's natural understanding of it.

"Can you really?"

Freya smiles, and lets Inga ask her for a curse.

"What will it do?" Inga asks when it is done, the magic laid under her skin like a tracery of fine silver wires. "How will I know if it works?"

"It will work." Freya smooths her hands over her foster sister's shoulders. "No man could stray from someone as beautiful as you, could fall in love with another, and no woman would fly away from her life with a man she has promised to love for always." The curse is sharp as bramble thorns. The prince will never love his trophy wife, he is merely in love with his reflection in her. Should he truly ever fall in love he will no longer be a man, but a beast. A hunting beast of the forest, a horror, an abomination. And if Inga is ever to leave the cage she has built for herself, she will become a bird and die a bird's little death.

One corner of Freya's mouth curls upward. It's only fitting, she tells herself. It's what they deserve.

Perhaps Inga is not as slow and stupid at magic as Freya has always assumed. She narrows her eyes and takes Freya's wrists in her long and delicate fingers. "Should I lose my prince," she says, and Freya feels the hooks and claws of Inga's spell catching at her sinews, digging into her bones, "you will take the form of a raven white and be bound to me in his place for all eternity. Your freedom will come only when you lose what you love most."

The two women step apart from each other, their teeth bared.

"So be it," says Freya.

Years pass, and nothing changes. The old king and his wife die, and the prince and his pretty Inga take their place. They have a little son, an heir who grows spoiled and wild under the long shadows of the castle.

Freya herself takes a suitor. A man she barely cares for, but he gives her a daughter before he leaves, and she keeps the girl as close to her as she can, never letting her leave the sanctuary of the deepest heart of the forest. She weaves spells around the Within, cocooning it in magic. In protection.

Even this is not enough, and Freya's daughter escapes her mother's clinging confines and runs far from the icy forest, following the sun, and the promise of freedom. The thing that was once Freya's heart beats slower and colder.

Time slips strange, long and short and in between, and Freya and Inga begin to forget. Their children have grown to adulthood, and nothing has ever happened. The prince is a king, and the head of the white hart still watches the hall while cobwebs gather in its antlers. The king's other trophy is perhaps less beautiful, but she has been tempered by the years, and so has the king. For the first time, he has begun to see her as a person, as someone who makes him laugh at spilled milk and bruised fruit. She in turn has begun to so see him as just a man, with flaws and facets to fascinate.

Curses are not bound by time or memory.

The day the king becomes a beast, the day the man falls in love, Freya knows it. She is deep in the heart of the forest – the Within that is hers and hers alone – when the pain reshapes her body. Her feet turn to claws and her arms are jerked out of shape and rearranged. She is shrouded in feathers, and like a fine chain, she feels the magic pulling her through the skies to Inga's windowsill at the very top of the castle. It is already deserted, the servants have fled. In the courtyard, the prince-that-was prowls the flag stones, his great claws raking gashes through the pitted stone.

"What have you done?" Inga says through gritted teeth.

The raven caws, flicks its white feathers. "What I promised. He is no man." She thinks of the daughter she loves, long since fled from the Within, and hopes that her runaway child will stay safe.

Inga presses her lips into a thin line, and tightens her grip on the ledge so that her finger bones show whitely beneath her thin skin. Her hands are beginning to age, just a little, and Freya can see wrinkles gathering at the corners of her eyes. Fine threads of silver weave between the gold of her hair. "And what happens if I leave this monster now, tell me?"

"You will become a little bird. You will have no more brains or heart than a wren." The raven bows. "And then you will die."

For a long moment Inga says nothing. She smiles instead, her eyes far away. Her smile is terrible. "And my son?"

"Send him away," Freya says, and for the first time she feels regret.

Not even Inga's curse strikes so deep. The boy is an innocent but even innocents will be caught in curses. "Send him far from magic and mystery and true love."

Inga closes her eyes. "There is no place far enough for him to run from love."

"Out of the forest, into the world of science and now. There he will be safe from curses."

"He will hate me, he will not understand," Inga says, and Freya's broken heart breaks more because she has done this to the ones she thought to hold dearest.

"Better to hate you, better to hate everyone," Freya says softly and they both look to the beast below, "than to be a man who falls in love."

"Or his keeper."

The first snow has begun to drift from the clouds and far below, the beast roars into the flurry and the falling night. The curses work their way deeper and Freya knows she must turn her heart to stone and forget her daughter. She must stay a raven and belong only to Inga so that the girl can live.

She bows her head and wills her mind to empty itself of regret. She has an eternity to serve out.

Another prequel story, this time for my novel Beastkeeper. Beastkeeper *revolves around a girl trying to break the curse on herself and her family, and "Counter Curse" is the story of how that curse came into being. It's about sisters, love and hate, cruelty and regret.*

Mouse Teeth

At seventeen, Elsie de Jager suffered a gum infection and the dentist had to pull every single tooth out of her head, collapsing her mouth before it ever had the chance to bloom. Of course, Dokter Marais had said there was nothing else for it, that there was no saving the teeth, and everyone in Flora agreed that it was a terrible thing, a terrible thing to happen to a young girl, and she'd been so pretty before that, they said. But Elsie knew it wasn't disease that took her teeth.

When she was seven, she'd baited one of Ouma's wood-and-steel traps with a little ivory point of a baby tooth, like a tiny fat dagger, and placed it under her narrow bed. When the crack had come, deep in the middle of the Free State night, she'd heard the scream as it died – a thin, vicious squeal.

Elsie had buried the dead tooth mouse. Not in Ma's barren yard, where the red-brown dust was swept smooth every morning under the sawing teeth of the outside broom. Instead she'd carried the little body wrapped in an old cotton handkerchief of her father's, and taken it out of the town, to where those English sisters lived, and buried it under a wiry tussock by their mailbox. It was a game the children played – primitive wardings to keep the English witches' eyes from them, to keep them safe.

One of the boys in her class claimed to have buried a stillborn sheep by the box, but Elsie didn't believe him. Her fingers turned the hard red dirt, easing a space between the grass roots for the little body. There was nothing buried there that she could see. No cats' bones or fragile corpses. She patted the soil down, and felt a tremor under her palms. Elsie pulled her hands away and glanced fearfully at the cottage. The air hummed around her as the bees from the sisters' hive watched, and Elsie had hurried back home as quickly as she could.

In Flora, everyone spoke Afrikaans, even the black labourers. When Elsie did hear the sisters speak in town sometimes, it made her prick her ears – such a slippery, trickster language, full of stolen sounds and mismatched vowels. And, of course, the English were evil. They'd stolen the land, and the gold and the freedom. They'd built concentration camps for women and children, and put glass in the porridge of infants. It made complete sense to Elsie that English was the language of witchcraft. Of evil. What else would it be?

But now she was eighteen, and she'd been to boarding school and she could speak accented English through her neat and painful vulcanite teeth, and give people neat and painful smiles. It was almost as if she was English herself. The man she'd married wasn't. Elsie wondered if she'd been cursed. Living in a town with an English name, when the dusty, empty Orange Free State was loosely scattered with towns with real names, proper names, commemorating the fallen dead. Strong names, farmer's names, where they had slowed their wagons and loosed their oxen.

It was a trial then, to grow up in Flora and to be almost-but-not-quite Afrikaans, and be married at eighteen with no teeth to an almost-but-not-quite farmer. Elsie knew this, and at night, after wiping herself clean of her husband's needs, she fumbled her dentures out in the tiny bathroom and cleaned them with her special brush and paste then left them in a clear tumbler, where they grinned at her like imbecilic reminders of her ill luck.

She would wake every morning at four so that she could set her teeth back in and make strong black coffee on the stove, and drink two cups before the man woke. Elsie was bleary-eyed, jaw-aching as the teeth settled (they never did, truly.) Instead they remained a constant vice-like ache, biting into her gums in punishment for that broken back, that last gasp of *merde!*)

Or perhaps the mouse had screamed murder. Elsie didn't know anymore. Perhaps the mouse had never screamed at all. The sun was just beginning to drizzle through the net curtains and, in the dawn light, Elsie saw there was still blood on the kitchen floor, caught in the little channels between the big raw-red tiles.

She looked to the closed kitchen door; it hadn't moved, so Gideon was still asleep. She had time. With a damp rag clutched in her bony fingers, Elsie got down on her knees and scrubbed at the flaking dried blood. Here and there little beads of it had gathered stickily in the corners, but soon they were also washed away, and the night's offering vanished.

If her kitchen floor had become the altar where nightly Gideon bled himself for his god, Elsie was no priestess. The kitchen was a violated shrine. It should have been offerings of malva-pudding and steaming maize porridge with cream and butter, or tripe cooked slowly with beans and tomatoes, for some fat and happy goddess.

Not human blood. Not Gideon screaming and crying and telling her that they would starve, that he was going to lose this job too.

The god of Kerkstraat wasn't listening. Last night had been worse than normal – Gideon asking her what would she do without him. That if he went, there would be no one to take care of her. Cutting his arms to show how he suffered, like a glimpse into the hell the dominee told them was waiting for them if they strayed from godliness to sin.

One day, Elsie thought, one day he would cut too deep, and when they took his corpse, everyone would know that he wasn't fit for Heaven. Elsie rolled the kitchen knives away in a chequered dishcloth, and put them in her outside bag. Then she went to the bathroom, and took the Mercurochrome bottle from the medicine cabinet and made sure its lid was screwed on tight, before adding that to her bag. Gideon's razor was resting on one of the narrow glass shelves in the cabinet, next to his shaving brush and his shaving bowl with its sliver of soap cradled like a natal scrap. She could have taken the razor too, of course, but that would have pointed a mocking finger at his terror. Elsie had grown up knowing that men did not like to have their flaws recognised, especially the flaws they thought were womanly and hysterical, bloody like monthly flow and filled with salt-sick tears.

The coffee Elsie left for him on the stove.

Her heart was fluttering with something that veered between fear and excitement. She was turning her back on God, she knew, by going to witches. They were abominations, they should be stoned, be beaten and burned. But they were women, and they were fat with women's secrets, like spiders in their webs. It didn't take long to reach the English sisters' house. Flora was a small town, neatly bisected by Kerkstraat, dividing the godly from the ungodly. The sisters lived on the side of sin, with the shops and the butchers and the women who sewed all through the night.

Elsie walked with her head held high, though it was early, and only a few old ladies had ventured out to sweep their empty front yards emptier in case the dominee should pass. It was a Sunday, so people would be getting ready to eat a full breakfast and suit themselves into their smart clothes. Then, with heads bowed and pious faces empty and barren as their dirt yards, they would walk down to the end of Kerkstraat, file into that dark building and begin to pray.

Elsie surprised a small flock of scavenging bosveld fisant, and the birds ran off ahead of her, kraaaing like fat old ladies shocked by something vulgar. The air was clear and cold, morning air before morning had fully woken, and Elsie breathed in deep with each swing of her arms. She wanted her lungs to be full, as if she was about to hold her head underwater.

The sisters' house came into view. It was smaller than she remembered as a child, a little tin-roof box with a garden kept clipped and green. Waste of water, Elsie thought. There were roses, fat-headed and drooping, and they smelled like Tannie Issie's perfumed Sunday best, and Elsie felt a prick in the corners of her eyes, as if bees had stung her blind. It took her a moment before she could walk on, past the little chicken-fence gate. More flowers were growing between the rose bushes. Elsie didn't know what they were called, most of them.

She stood on their stoep, assaulted by the sweetness of the English garden, and covered her mouth with one hand, her tongue pressing at the backs of her dentures, until she was certain everything was straight, before she knocked at the door. Her shoes were small and pointed, and made her feet hurt, church best against the ragged stoep paint, and Elsie stared at them until the door creaked open, and a round-faced woman peered blearily out at her. Elsie wasn't sure which one this was, Catherine or Elizabeth.

When Elsie was seven, the sisters had seemed severe and ancient. Now, at eighteen, she realised this one, at least, was small and soft, and only about fifteen years older than she was.

"Elsie de Jager," the woman said without surprise, as if she were used to strangers arriving unannounced on her stoep at five on a Sunday morning.

"Snyman," Elsie said automatically. "It's Elsie Snyman now. I married Hendrik Snyman's son."

"Gideon or Theunis?" the woman asked. Then she closed her eyes. "What does it matter, Elizabeth? Stop talking nonsense and let the poor girl in."

She opened her eyes again, wide and startled like a little witkoluil, and stepped back to beckon Elsie into her house. Even the way she bobbed her head reminded Elsie of an owl.

Elsie murmured her thanks and put one foot firmly over the threshold. She wasn't sure what she expected in a house of English witches, but the sisters' little cottage was neat and simple, and there were handmade doilies on the small couch, just like in her own house. Elsie felt a little disappointed. A round-bellied black stove sulked in the corner, but it was too small to burn a child in, unless perhaps they squeezed a newborn into that little mouth. Perhaps there were tiny bones in the ash they scraped out. They had a wall full of books, so that at least was different.

"Catherine, dear," Elizabeth called. "We've a visitor." She turned back to Elsie. "Sit down, Miss de Jager, and I'll bring you some tea."

She wanted to point out (again) that she was married now, with a married woman's stamp of authority, and that she preferred coffee, because that was a real drink. It put hairs on your chest. Elsie swallowed the words like a mouthful of bees and, surprisingly, she felt better for it. They warmed up her stomach.

The other sister appeared from the back of the house. She was older and taller than Elizabeth, and it gave her a more stately look – a goshawk to her sister's owl. Her hair was greying and pinned back neatly in careful curves. It looked like she'd been up and dressed since before the moon had set, and Elsie wondered if they'd been awake all night, chanting and dancing, leaving sacrifices to English gods they'd brought with them in their trunks. Celtic goddesses they'd wrapped in the broken wings of fairies, garlanded with flowers that wouldn't grow here in this arid place.

"It's not often we get visitors," said Catherine, coolly. "To what do we owe such an honour?"

"Oh for heaven's sake, Catherine, stop being such an immense drip. It's obvious the poor girl's been shaken up by something. And she wouldn't come to us unless it were a secret." Elizabeth bustled back into the front room, and set out a tray of pretty little cups and saucers, and a steaming pot of tea clad in a voluminous cosy. "You can tell us, dear," she said to Elsie. "We're used to it. We hear it all. The little secrets and the big ones."

Elsie swallowed. "What do you mean?" She'd thought her English remarkably good, but now here, against their shatter-bright tones, her words felt clipped at the edges, so that they came out the wrong shape, flattened and dull.

"They wouldn't be secrets if we told you," snapped Catherine, who Elsie was beginning to dislike in a fearful sort of way – the kind of dislike that was gilded with guilty admiration. She wanted to be sharp and snippy too. A falcon instead of a little dog with no teeth.

Elizabeth poured tea and milk for her, and stirred in sugar when Elsie asked. Finally, when all the three women had their porcelain shields in place, Elizabeth smiled at her, sipped once, and said, "You may begin, Elsie, dear."

Where did she start? Elsie thought. What could she say that didn't make a small thing sound bigger than it was? And it was a small thing, really, in the grand scheme of the world and the universe. "I think my husband is going to murder himself," she said.

Elizabeth set down her tea, and glanced at her older sister.

Catherine sighed. Finally she spoke. "Why do you think that?" Her voice had changed from beak and talon sharp. It was a careful voice now, one that was unpicking knots in silk.

Elsie cleared her throat with an embarrassed cough, and fumbled in her bag for the kitchen knives. She unrolled the dishcloth, and displayed the knives on the sisters' ornate table. "He uses these," she said, without looking up. The blades were old, but sharp. They had been her ouma's, given to her after the funeral. Some were so well used that the blades had become sickle smiles, almost thin enough to see through. "He uses these," she said again to the grinning silver. "Nightly, in the kitchen, and he cries for the Lord, but I do not think the Lord is listening."

A very long silence was punctuated by the long slow tick of the clock on the wall, and the faint drone of the bees as they worked the flowers outside the window.

"He will kill himself, eventually, yes," said Catherine. "And he will blame you for it, as men always blame their weaknesses on women. You will try stop him, playing your part as dutiful wife, and he will leave scars on your arms, and guilt in your heart."

Elsie shivered and bowed her head closer to her chest, trying not to cry in front of these Englishwomen. They were witches, seeing her future laid out like a poor man's feast – gristle and bone and empty dishes.

"What do you want us to do?" Elizabeth said kindly. "We cannot stop him."

"No," said Catherine, and Elsie looked up into her amber eyes. "I'm afraid that we cannot change what must be. We cannot avert the deaths to come, or change the shape of the heart."

Elizabeth nodded. "We cannot make love grow, and we cannot rip death out by the root. We cannot change one flower into another, not forever, anyway."

"Then what can you do?" said Elsie. "What use are you?"

Catherine stood. "We can save you from wasted time." She went to the long bookcase, and opened one of the leaded-glass doors to take out a small box, like a cigar case. She brought the little case back to the table and handed it to Elsie, who took it, her eyebrows raised. "What is this thing?"

"Open it," said Catherine.

The box was small enough to balance easily on the palm of her hand. Faded lettering had been inked on the top. It was tin, the corners rusted, brown earth dry as old breadcrumbs caught in the hinges. Elsie struggled to open it, but finally the lid snapped back, and inside she found a small roll of cotton, carefully wrapped around a desiccated bundle of bones and skin.

"You left it for us," said Elizabeth, from the couch. She blinked once, slowly. "A powerful token. You must have had some natural skill. Oh, what we could have done with you if you'd been ours. What we could have taught you."

The mouse was ten years dead, held together by dust. Elsie pressed her tongue against her false teeth and swallowed. She closed the tin carefully. "What – what must I do with this?"

"Your man eats, doesn't he?" said Elizabeth, and Elsie recalled then that as round-faced and owl-eyed as she was, owls were still killers, breakers of bones, silent hunters. "Gideon or Theunis or whatever son he is, they all eat. They never cook. Cooking is the witchcraft of women." She leaned forward and tapped the edge of the tin with one oval nail. "Grind it into his food."

Back at the house, Gideon was awake, drinking his coffee sweetened with condensed milk. "Where were you?" he said.

Elsie's heart shivered like a mouse before a cat pounced, and she smiled her neat and painful smile, her gums aching. "I needed antiseptic. We'd run out." She fished in her bag, careful not to touch the wrapped blades or the little tin mouse coffin, and drew out a glass bottle. "I got some Mercurochrome from Sanet –"

"You didn't say what it was for," he said, his voice hard and scared and angry.

"No." Elsie set the small dark glass bottle down on the table, her hands shaking. "Of course not. I'll just get some bandages and we can clean you up properly before church. You don't want infection setting in." As though the cuts along his arms were accidents, a slip, it could happen to anyone.

When he was stained and covered, Elsie made breakfast. Porridge, milky and sweet, the oats soaked overnight, heated slow and sticky, smoothed out with salted butter and the cream from the top of the milk. The mouse she ground down in her herb mortar, and Elsie stirred the dust of its bones into his bowl, before sprinkling a crust of brown sugar over. She brought him his breakfast in the dining room, and they ate in silence, heads bowed before the grace of God.

That night, after Elsie had taken out her teeth and polished them and scoured every line and dip, and drowned them in cold water, she tiptoed to bed in the dark, her mouth sunken and soft. She lay straight as a new sapling next to Gideon, and listened to him sleep. The sounds he made were soft and furry, and Elsie put one hand to her breast and felt her heart beating under her palm, until the sound of it filled her ears and her skull and pulsed her bones like a drum. She wanted to dance to that beat, to shake off her nightdress and run naked through the night, taste the stars like white bees. Swallow mouthfuls of them until she was stung back to life. Instead, she kept stiller than still, and fell asleep, her skin shrouded in thick flannel.

In her dreams, she walked the passage of the house Gideon Snyman had bought her with his share of the Snyman inheritance. He'd given up his claim to the farm in order to have a share of the money early. He'd wanted to impress his bride, the most beautiful girl in Flora – or she would have been, if her teeth hadn't all been pulled out.

The floors were dark beneath her bare feet, and Elsie looked down at the smooth, silky wood in surprise. She never walked barefoot, that freedom lost to childhood. But there were her feet, white and plain. She'd never had pretty feet, just solid, peasant ones. Boere-feet. Feet that could walk for miles, feet that were narrowed by shoes so that they would look neater, adult and proper. Her toes lengthened, the nails turning into sharp claws that tacked along the wood. Elsie the dog with no teeth. She growled, and the dreaming Elsie turned over in her sleep and pressed one hand against her husband's spine.

Head down, Elsie sniffed along the edges of the passage, nosing the trail of twisting scents that zipped and zagged and jumped and popped along the skirting boards. Mice. The house had never had mice before, and the little terrier wagged the stump of its tail in delight, ready for a hunt.

It didn't take long for the trail to lead her to the mouse. It sat on its back legs, blatant and uncaring, on the dinner table, stuffing its bewhiskered face with food. There were dishes all over the table, left uncleared, the food half-eaten, and the gravy congealing in oily lumps. Elsie leapt up onto one of the chairs, and placed her front paws on the table.

The mouse paused, and looked once at the terrier, before resuming its gluttony.

"You should be scared of me," Elsie said.

"Scared?" The mouse threw down the maize kernel it had been nibbling. "Of a little dog with no teeth? I don't think so."

And Elsie knew it was right, could feel the useless slobbery gums that were all she had. She couldn't eat the softest food without pain. How was she to snap up this little intruder?

She whined softly and sunk her head onto the table.

Her jaw ached.

In her marital bed, Elsie twisted, turned away from her husband and curled up, her knees against her stomach. She pressed her hands against her empty mouth and wept in her sleep, soaking the pillows with salt.

On the dining room table, the terrier ground its jaws, feeling the splinter sharp pain as new teeth, fat and pointed, tore through the soft gums.

The mouse froze.

Upstairs, Elsie overslept. She slept through the rising sun and the bells from the distant station. She slept through the milk van, and the clatter of hooves as one of the labourers drove his cart through the town main road.

She slept curled up around herself, while at her back, her husband cooled.

It was near noon when she woke. Gideon didn't stir, though Elsie watched him for a long time. In a daze, she dressed, and walked to the police station, her tongue pressed against the tiny ivory pegs in her mouth. She spoke to the constable dully.

"I overslept."

"He was like that when I woke."

"No, I don't know what happened."

When she got back home, late, so late in the afternoon that the sun was turning the few trees on the road into red sentinels, Elsie stared at her reflection in the bathroom mirror. They had taken the body away, made notes of the cuts on his arms.

"Woodworking accident," Elsie had told them.

Her vulcanite dentures grinned at her from their tumbler, like exhibits in a museum.

Elsie de Jager bared her teeth in the mirror. They were small and fat and new. Children's teeth.

Tomorrow she would catch a train to Bloemfontein, and from there to Cape Town. She would learn English properly, and to play tennis, and to drink lemon-tea and gin, and the names of flowers, and how to use mouse bones for magic, and she would call herself Elizabeth.

"Mouse Teeth" is based on my own family. My grandfather tried to kill his family with a shotgun, then overdosed on arsenic. While I think my grandmother did try to reinvent herself, she never really managed to break free of her past. This story was my chance to envision a world where she escaped to make her own way in a world that was less cruel to her. Names have been changed to protect the guilty dead.

A Sun Bright Prison

The problem with selkies is they stink. Even the half-castes have that rotten fish smell. It clings to them like a curse.

Out past the very oldest parts of town, past the newly-gentrified Whelker's Quarter, there are still families with selkie blood. They barely qualify as magical. Only the slightest touch of seal – there's no way to tell what they are just by looking at them.

The only way to know is by that pervasive stink of fish.

That's what I've been told my whole life and I've always accepted it as fact. Vamps smell of old blood and spoiled milk and new-printed money, and selkies smell like the fish market at the end of the day. That's what we said about the boy in our class, back when we were still stamping out our place in the school hierarchy; parroting our parents, our peers, the crowd we wanted to impress.

This is the first time I've ever been up close to him, though. Pressed behind him in the queue to hand in our registration papers.

He was in my classes all through primary and high school, and I've pretty much ignored him the way he's ignored everyone else. I mean, I get that I'm ugly and odd-looking and I wear spectacles and that makes me untouchable, but he's worse. And sitting with him at break would have damned me for my entire school career. So, callous little cow that I was, all caught up in my own self-pitying selfishness, I joined in when they called him fish-breath and half-breed and teased him about losing his skin.

So cruel. I ache now when I think about it.

I wonder if he knows that I'm standing right behind him, surreptitiously trying to see if he smells like the harbour. I breathe in deeply, but all I get is that boy-smell of sweat and skin, musk... is that fish?

He shifts, and I draw back a little.

"Forge," he says without turning around, his voice very low, pitched so that only I can hear him. "Would it help if I raised an arm or something? Then you could shove your face right into my armpit."

Saints. "I don't know what you're talking about," I whisper back, horrified that anyone around us will overhear. The long queues of soon-to-be students are buzzing with talk, and I don't think anyone is paying us the slightest attention, but still. My face has gone hot. Stupid selkie.

"No?" He turns around, smiles at me. His teeth are very white, but skew. His eyes are blacker than sea depths. There's nothing obviously selkie about him. Then again, how would I know? It's not like he ever talked about his family or anything. Or that we ever took the time to ask him. "Then what exactly are you trying to do?"

"Nothing." I hug my enrolment forms against my chest. Illustration and design, because there's nothing else. It's not as if I come from one of the old families who run Pelimburg and who go to the university to harness their bonds and magics and whatever they do. All I get is college. I mean, technically, anyone can marry a vamp and bond and... stuff, but it's not as if Nadena Forge went to the right parties or lived in the right neighbourhood. "Handing in my forms."

The smile is gone. Not like it was a real smile, anyway. "Nadena – you're the arty girl, right? That's what you're studying?"

I nod slowly. "Yeah." I sent in my portfolio months ago, all this stuff now is just filling in the required nonsense for my student ID so I have access to the campus and all that. I'm also supposed to pick up the first-year supplies. Which I have to carry home with me on the omnibus, so that's going to be all kinds of wonderful. "And you," I try out his name, the first time I've actually used it in over a decade of knowing him, "Ridlea?" See, it doesn't help if you're half-monster and your parents go and saddle you with a name like that.

"And me, what?"

"Studying."

"Oh." Ridlea looks down at his own papers, as if he's somehow forgotten. "History," he says, which could mean anything. "Language." He looks vaguely embarrassed, like I've caught him in a lie.

"Which one is it?"

He doesn't answer. One of the women dealing with paperwork is sighing loudly and gesturing at her desk, and Ridlea gives me a half smile before going up and dumping his forms in front of her. The other woman at the counter is stamping the last of a red-headed girl's papers, and I'll be next. Our conversation is over. Twelve years in the same schools and this is the first time I realise that Ridlea really doesn't smell like fish.

I'm up to my ears in projects. We've had a few excursions to galleries and private exhibitions – one of the perks of studying art – and on one memorable occasion we spent an entire day sketching some of the rarer magical beasts still in captivity. The collection was housed underground and the beasts mostly reptilian. They watched us from behind thick glass, their scales lit by the eerie yellow light. They don't belong in our world any more. We keep them safe behind iron-edged cases, and they lie in their own shit while we draw them.

Today, our life-drawing instructor has apparently given up on trying to herd students and sent us off on our own into the city to practice doing quick ink sketches of people. I've found a relatively quiet tea-shop doing outdoor trade. The day is pleasant, the sun bright, the air sea-cool, and for a change, not windy. Maybe our instructor just wanted to enjoy the good weather rather than be cooped up in a dull brick prison with a bunch of barely-talented magicless commoners. I don't exactly blame her.

My portfolio case is positioned as discreetly under the table as I can manage, I have a pot of tea as cover, and I'm using my smallest sketch book. I could be any student making notes. Instead, I am spying. That's what it feels like. I'm drawing the couple sitting at the high table, their pale faces shaded by the lemon-yellow umbrella. The girl looks bilious. The guy looks... vampish. Definitely. Surprising that they're out this far into Old Town. Ever since Pelim Allegria married a Sandwalker and declared herself Empress of Oreyn, the vamps and their partners have become the new elite, separated from us by their magic and their power.

A few people are looking at the couple sidelong and whispering, but they seem not to care, pretending that they can't hear us.

What's one more person staring? I scribble their faces, the way their arms almost touch, the angles of their bodies, how they tilt toward each other as if there are no other people in the universe. For them, there probably aren't. They have magic, and that puts them in a different world to people like me. We're chaff. Dispensable.

My pen splats ink, and I try work the unexpected spill into a shadow. That's part of being an artist – working mistakes to your advantage.

"You're good," says a man behind me. His voice is low and soft, and it walks hand in hand with blackthorn eyes and crooked teeth. I know this without looking, and the thought makes me feel stupid and slow, ridiculous.

I pull a napkin over my sketch and turn around to face him. Ridlea. I haven't seen him on campus, but then again I'm on the far side; the art department, where the freaks and wild-haired gather. The ones who hint at magic in their blood as if somehow it makes them better. "Hasn't anyone ever told you it's rude to look over someone's shoulder?"

Ridlea slides into the chair opposite me and sets his bag between his feet. He's blocking my view of the vamp and his... whatever. "No. Just as no one ever told you it's weird and creepy to draw complete strangers without their permission."

"Please. That's not creepy."

"It is, a little."

"Besides, it's their own fault for coming down here where they're so," I wave one hand, "visible."

"Visible?" He echoes, and raises one eyebrow.

"Yeah, flaunting their magic."

"How are they flaunting anything?" He turns in his seat, peering back at the couple. "Or should they stay hidden because they have something you don't have?" He settles back, stares at me.

That's not what I meant at all. It's not about them flaunting their magic, it's them shoving their status in our faces and expecting us to treat them differently. And what have they done for us, anyway? Besides change the path of our country completely. Since they came into power, we're back on trading terms with the Mekekana. We've got machinery, steel and circuitry in the Old Town. If the old Lammer Houses still ruled, we'd still be stuck with copper and glass and bone. Just like the way Pelim's Leap has preserved itself – an island of magical elitism that clings to the things of the past.

The more I think about how to explain myself, the more petulant it sounds. Small and jealous. I narrow my eyes. "No lectures today?"

"Only morning classes. I'm supposed to be in the library, studying." He leans over to order a pot of tea from the waitress, then turns his attention back to me. "Is this for school?" He says it like that, school. As if we're both still children.

"Life-drawing." I snap my sketchbook closed, cap my pen, and slip them both away into my portfolio, which pretty much doubles as a waste-paper basket and giant stationery bag because I am not the tidiest person in the world. I take a sip of cold tea.

Seems today is all about magic, about the unexplainable. Vampires in the tea-houses. Selkies studying for exams. We sit facing each other, and I let myself look at him, wondering if the rumours and the insults have even the tiniest grain of salty truth to them. He's dark enough to be part-selkie, slick as a fur-seal, and this time.... I try not to be obvious, breathing in deeply.

"I had a fish roll," he says. "For lunch."

"Urgh," I say. I feel like an over-ripe tomato, red and putridly sweaty. "I wasn't –"

"Of course you were." He flicks his fingernails against the porcelain of his tea cup, then pauses to glance up at me. "You could just ask, you know." He sounds tired and bitter.

"Fine." I push my disgusting cold tea away from me. "If you want people to not think you're weird, maybe leave out the fish rolls and go for something normal, such as an ice cream."

He flashes a glimpse of crooked teeth and I wish I still had my sketchbook out and I could pin him into my memory with quick black lines. "Maybe next time. Come on, ask your stupid question."

I sigh, but my heart is a starling flutter of wings under my ribs. "Are you a selkie? Or you know. Part – you know what I mean."

"You can't be part-selkie," Ridlea says.

"Of course you can – if your mother –"

"Father," he says. "But no, I know what you mean, but you're wrong. A selkie is a selkie. That's it. I'm human. I don't have a spare skin floating around that I use to transform myself into a seal."

We're both quiet for a little while. "But your father does," I say softly. The thought is bizarre. I've always pictured selkies as being women who fell for brutish fishermen, who had their skins stolen from them and were trapped in loveless marriages. I never thought of boy-selkies.

Ridlea nods.

This is so weird. "Does he still – I mean, is he still around?"

"You're nosier than you were in school. I'm not sure if I prefer this or if I think you should go back to calling me fish-breath."

My flush, which I'd just managed to get under control, comes sweeping over me again. "Oh saints, that – I am so sorry. Children are cruel."

"You're still a child," Ridlea says. "So am I. Do you really think a handful of exams and a few months have made us all grow up?" But he's wrong. Because I don't think Ridlea's ever been just a child. We never let him be.

"I'm still sorry," I mumble.

"Don't worry about it," he says. "I'll introduce you to my father."

I have no idea why I agreed. We catch two omnibuses out past the Whelker's Quarter, towards the east where the land is flat and scrubby and the houses all resemble little tan barnacles hugging the ground. It's quiet here, much quieter than Old Town where the college is and where I've grown up. The wind blows in off the rolling ocean, picking up litter and tossing it in the air.

The place feels like another world; it's impossible to see Pelimburg properly, just the hazy blue of the cliffs. This was dumb. Anything could happen to me. He could kill me and dump my body. No one knows where I am.

"It's a little bit of a walk from the stop," Ridlea says. "So when you get tired, give me that." He points to my portfolio.

The strap is already digging into my shoulder, but I ignore the offer. "Thanks, but I'm fine." Almost twenty minutes later I'm rather regretting it, and I don't even pretend to hide a sigh of relief when we turn up a little seagrass-edged road and Ridlea swings open the small ramshackle wooden gate of a tiny yard. Nothing grows in here, just sand. Is this a place where magic can live? A wild place, far from iron and smoke.

"Dad?" Ridlea says when he opens the door, calling out softly into the shadowy quiet. The house smells clean and lemony, and the walls are painted white. Everything is very neat. "Dad, sorry I'm late. Do you want tea?"

The house doesn't answer. "Set your bag down and take a seat," Ridlea ushers me into the kitchen and before I have a chance to protest he's hauling out bread and making sandwiches. There's a wooden icebox in one corner, and I realise with a start that obviously they would have to use old things. No modern conveniences for his father.

His dad might not be high born or anything, but he's still a selkie. Still magic. Iron must hurt them as much as it does the old families and the vamps. But selkies don't get to live in glass palaces.

Ridlea fillets some small fish and mushes them onto a slice of bread while I look around, and try not to be obvious about it. The kitchen is filled with copper and wood and glass and porcelain. The house is stone and wood, the roof thatched. "Can he not be around iron?" I ask very softly, in case Ridlea's invisible dad might hear.

"This way," Ridlea says, and takes the fish sandwich and a glass of what smells like yeasty beer. I follow him out of the kitchen, past the unlit lounge, and through to a small back room, mostly encased in glazed windows. A slight man is sitting on a worn couch with a blanket thrown over his knees.

"Dad?" Ridlea sets the sandwich and beer down on the little side table, but the man seems not to notice. He's dark, thin, almost starved-looking, and he stares out the window to where the thin blue line of the ocean is just visible. The corners of his black eyes are webbed with fine wrinkles, and his hair is short and slick-looking, dark and somehow silvery at the same time. "Dad, I've brought a friend who wanted to meet you."

A friend.

A tourist, more like. I shuffle my feet. "Hello, Mr. Leverin." That's who Ridlea has been to me. Leverin. Only a few teachers ever called him by his first name, as they did the rest of us. "I'm Nadena, I go to college with Ridlea."

The man doesn't move.

Ridlea tugs gently at my sleeve, and I follow him out of the little sun room.

We're back in the kitchen. Ridlea is making us tea, boiling up water in a copper kettle. Everything must take so long here. I think of my own house with all its bright modern plastics and steels, all the things trade with the Mekekana has brought us. In comparison, Ridlea's house feels primitive. I guess magic is. It's deeper and older and it doesn't like change. "Your dad – is he ill?"

"He's been like that for years. I'm used to it. He's not ill, just been in one shape for too long, too far from water."

I don't know if I should ask the obvious, but then again, I've already stepped into his world and soured it with my stupid questions.

"Can he go back?" Oh saints, maybe he can't because Ridlea's mother burned his skin or something, or locked it away where he'll never find it. This is so uncomfortable. "Forget I asked," I blurt out. "That was stupid –"

"It's in the hall closet," Ridlea says. "The skin."

Oh. So why doesn't he just leave? I can't bring myself to ask.

But Ridlea starts talking as if he knows all the questions brimming in my head, and he keeps talking and maybe he's waited all this time for someone to tell, because he needed to make sense of it and none of us ever cared and all we did was call him fish-breath and sealskin. "It's not like in the stories – she didn't steal his skin away and trap him. He gave it to her. They're in love, or they were I guess. I mean, they still are, they sit and hold hands together and my mom tells him all about her day, even though he never speaks.

"They weren't always like this. He used to be good, used to take us down to the sea and we'd get ice creams and sometimes he'd even slip his old skin on and change for us and it was normal. And then, slowly, he just started going out less and less and he didn't want to change and then after a while – this."

He stands up and musses his dark hair. "She keeps telling him to go back. She even used to leave his skin on the bed when she left for work each morning. I think she hoped that he'd go back even if it broke her heart."

"She stopped?"

"It – he said it made him too sad to see the skin, so now she just keeps it in the closet and she doesn't ask him or anything but..." He sighs and sits down again. "She took him down to the beach a few weeks ago – hired a driver and everything."

"What did he do?"

Ridlea snorts softly. "Nothing. Sat and looked at the water for a while, then asked what we were having for supper."

There's nothing to say. I fold my hands on the table and look at the wood. He's telling me all these things like we've been friends all our lives, and I have no idea how to react or what to say. My glasses slowly slide down my nose, and I push them back up, but I don't look at him. It's getting too embarrassing, too personal. I want to be back home. I'm late already.

"He's going to die like this," Ridlea says. His voice is very small. A child's voice in this old-fashioned kitchen.

"I should get going," I say. "I should be home by now."

"I've weirded you out." His lopsided bitter smile is back. "Fucking half-breeds, right?"

"It's not – I really am late, my parents will worry."

"I thought you weren't a child anymore." He pushes up from the table abruptly. "Never mind, you're right. I'll catch the bus back with you, you'll be fine."

I don't see Ridlea around campus after that, not for the next few months and I'm so caught up in upcoming project deadlines and stupid little class-rivalries that mostly I don't even think about him much.

When I do, it's late at night and I can't sleep, and I wonder what it would be like to have a boy kiss me, touch me, and I use my fingers and pinch my nipples and stifle the noise I make and thank all the saints that the new house means I no longer have to share a room with my younger sister.

I'm being stupid. I don't even know why I think about him. After all, it's not as if we have any romantic moments to build on. It makes no sense. My mother asks me if I've "met someone," with a knowing smirk and I haven't. It annoys me that she thinks I have.

I'm in the college cafeteria, desperately putting the final touches to an illustration project I'm supposed to hand in today, when I see him again. He's bought himself a greasy meal wrapped in wax paper, and he's slowly unfolding it at a far table. For some reason, I am entranced by his fingers, by his bowed head. He's sitting alone.

"An actual fish-breath," says one of my class mates next to me. He's short, angry about everything, studying to be a designer. "That's what I heard, anyway."

"A what?" I mumble, and grab a red pen to fix a line. It doesn't quite match the paint I used and makes the whole thing look even worse. I should have just left well alone.

"Over there." He points at the hunch-backed figure of Ridlea. "Part-selkie. Believe it or not."

I shove all my pens back into their bag and push my illustration over. "Hand this in for me, please."

"What?"

"There are no part-selkies." I get up and sling my portfolio half-over my shoulder and walk over to Ridlea.

"Hey," I say, though I don't sit down.

He peers up at me, and he's not as attractive as I remember him at night. His nose is too broad, his eyes too close together. It doesn't matter.

"Everything all right?" I squint. He really does look worse, like everything's been sucked out of him. "No fish rolls today?"

"My father died," he says, and I drop my portfolio onto one foot.

After a while, during which I think of everything that I should say or could have said, I settle on: "I'm sorry."

"Why? He wasn't anyone to you."

"Because I – I'm sorry you're sad." I bite my lip at the mediocrity of sentiment. "Are you –" Not all right, that's stupid, of course he's not all right. "Do you have class now?"

He stares at me. "In a few minutes, yes."

"Ditch it."

Ridlea picks at his half-eaten roll. "Fine," he says. "Why not?" But it's so limp and empty that I wonder if he doesn't have a skin of his own somewhere, put away and forgotten.

He doesn't say anything, doesn't ask me where we're going. Even when we reach the long stretch of muddy sand that marks the closest beach to Old Town, his expression doesn't change.

I make him take off his boots and socks, roll up his trousers. We walk silently in the shallows together, our feet turning blue and numb.

We hold hands, fingers shaking with the cold. The beach is empty except for a few die-hards and fishermen. There are no selkies.

Of course.

"What happened to his skin?"

Ridlea shrugs. "He left it to me."

My stomach does a little twist. I had expected him to say they'd buried him in it, or burned it in a ceremony or something. I don't really understand magic. I didn't think it got handed down like a family heirloom.

"Can you –?" I take another step deeper into the ocean like I'm dragging him in, and a small wave swells up my thighs, soaking my trousers and the bottom of my shirt.

"Yes."

We don't say anything after that, but our hands tighten, fingers pressing so close that I imagine we will burn right through to the bones and meld together. The sea mews flock overhead, twisting in the air currents like reflections of the schools of fish below them. I'm shivering hard now despite the heat from the sun. The water is freezing, clawing at me, dragging the sand out from under my feet.

"You should go back," I tell him, my voice lower than the hushing of the cold waves. Back – back to a place he never came from. How can he go back?

"Yes," he says, and in that moment I know he won't. That he will hand his skin on to some girl and that he will pine away for a family he does not know, for a world he was never part of.

It is cold and lonely here on the edge of the ocean, but the sun is out, and the water catches the light in silvery-bright cups. There is no point standing here and watching the endless heaving nothing of the world Ridlea never asked for, and will now never be able to completely let go.

There will always be some magicless person chaining him in place. What strange pretty prisons we build for ourselves. So the vampires have their palaces of glass and stone on the hills, the unicorns go to pasture in reservations where we can feed them little yellow apples. The wyrms lie in dank terrariums and shed empty papery skins.

Ridlea will fold the seal skin over a wooden hanger, hide it at the back of his closet behind the suit he bought for his father's funeral.

But today we have sun, and bright cold breezes that fill our lungs like bellows, and the sound of the vendor's handbells. "Ice cream," I say. "We should get ice creams."

Based in the same world as When the Sea is Rising Red, *this selkie story was set quite far in the future, where I was envisioning a new world made from the bones of the old. It's about prejudice, but it's also about wanting what you have instead of what you can never grasp.*

SEREIN

It's always about the ones who disappear.

I've imagined it endlessly: what Claire must have thought as she packed her bag. How leaving is easy, even if you lie and say 'oh god it's hard it's hard it's hard'. Make a clean break, leave everything, let loose your claim to possession: this is my house, this is my bed, these are my albums not shelved alphabetically because I tried and never could keep the world orderly, this is my little library built out of gifts and second-hand forgotten paperbacks.

This is my sheet ripe with me, this is my mirror, this is my reflection.

I close my sister's room. I don't know what she was thinking when she left.

I can pretend, for a while, that I felt her fear of life, her hurt. She said, always, *it will be better under water.* She would stay in the shower, drain the cylinder cold.

She took my mum's car when she left, though I suppose she gave it back. The police found it parked under a flyover near the airport, as if she'd driven up onto the verge and got out and walked on bleeding feet over broken glass to a pair of wings, to freedom. Other people in my town whispered that of course we'd love to think she caught a plane. There's no record of her from there. She took her passport, but didn't buy a ticket.

I married three years after Claire disappeared. And here's the thing. I have these pictures I hate to look at because no matter how much I smile in them, or how much money Mum and Dad pulled together to help me have the best wedding – the best wedding for their only daughter, their only child – no one can ignore that the photos are ruined. There are empty spaces where my sister should be, strange gaps where elbows don't meet, where heads cant, where shadows fall in the wrong direction. There are water stains that bubble like a strange mould between the layers of film.

He was a terrible photographer, our Uncle Jay. He's dead now, but he's still real. He has a plot, and a nice headstone. Mum goes to visit him now and again.

Cancer is a fucking destroyer; it took my mum's baby brother away from her, like a slice of her soul was excised.

I know how she feels about that. There are still photos of my sister in my mum's lounge. I'm here to help her clean. She's getting on in years, her and Dad, but they won't hire a char, not even to come in one day a week to help. Mum says she's never needed to hire anyone to do her cleaning for her and it won't start now.

So I come in, and do it for free while my daughter's in school.

My face twists. Mum is sleeping, lulled into childlike nap-time by the whine of the vacuum. I've stashed it away, and now I'm just faffing really, dusting knickknacks and photos that don't need dusting. I look at the ostrich feather duster held out like a wand, and wonder if I could summon my sister back. She's not dead. There's no proof of that.

The water in the vase of flowers sitting on the mantelpiece is rank, eddies stirring the greening muck, the flower heads sagging, spilling petals. Next to the curling pale fingers of a dead iris, my sister smiles uncertainly from a school portrait. She was wearing glasses, before she got her contact lenses and re-invented herself.

She would have hated this picture, hated knowing our mum kept it, right where visitors could have seen it and gone, "Is that your Claire, I never, she looks so different now!" which of course no one ever says because visitors never Talk About Claire. They talk about the rain, or who's doing what with whom. Claire's name has gone missing from people's minds.

I only remember it because every night before bed and after I've brushed my teeth, I lean in close to the bathroom mirror, until my breath fogs the silver, and write her name with my fingernail. Little scratches through water.

She drowned, people said after.

Where they think she managed that, I'd love to know. Did she walk barefoot (her shoes were left in the car, along with all her luggage – she certainly looked as if she'd packed to travel) for miles along the grey heels of the road, staggering through dusk and dawn, past the city houses, until she found a river wide enough to take her soul.

Fuck you, Claire.

It's not hard to leave.

It's hard to stay.

I spit on her photo, and the bubble of saliva slides tragically down her face. Not like a delicate tear, but an unwiped sneeze.

You have made me hate you.

No, no, not hate. I love, I always love, come back, Claire. I didn't mean it, we won't be angry, come back. Come back before Mum and Dad join Uncle Jay in the quiet plot, before I am too old to remember your name and write it in water.

When my sister Alison leaves, she closes the door on our mother, asleep, spittle hanging from her half-open mouth. She snores softly, sweetly as a baby. I saw Alison's baby born. Was there, drifting from water droplet to water droplet, I folded around her when she was still forming bridges between nerve and muscle, growing a liver, learning a heart. I was the sweat on my sister's forehead, I slid down her back, I pooled in her eyes. I know my sister more intimately than she knows herself.

This is not fear, or cowardice.

This is how to drown.

Take one brain bowed under the weight of its own unstoppable thoughts.

Take lungs that cannot stretch wide enough to fill with air. Because water is hard to come back from, because air is difficult, breathe smoke instead. It will give you wrinkles but make you beautiful. You will be a siren in a black-and-white film, your eyes filled with sex and knowledge.

This is power.

You will pack your bags with the things you cannot leave behind.

You will leave them behind at the end anyway, it doesn't matter.

You will drive in your mother's car; a fusty dry womb that smells of air-freshener and, faintly, of vomit. It is familiar. You will stick to the seats and roll the window down so you can smoke faster. You will play the same song on repeat and wish you were a child again.

Claire was always disappearing. Mum would give us some instruction on chores and as soon as her back was turned I'd be alone, having to clean our shared room all by myself. I'll give her this much, at least, she didn't make much mess if you ignored the bed-wetting.

She liked to be clean, Claire. Not just the endless showers, but she liked to have her world ordered. Her bed straight, her records alphabetised. Her books were packed as neatly as she could get them. She wasn't all about obsessively vacuuming or folding clothes, though, she could be filthy about some things, our Claire. I think she wanted the world to have a semblance of control, because she knew it was actually chaos.

It still annoyed me; the disappearing. When we were kids, she threw the biggest tantrum ever when Mum paid for us to have lessons at the local pool, so we wouldn't drown (in the middle of the city, far from water.)

Claire wet her bed, and the room smelled of urine, hot and sweet, even after Mum washed all the bedding; the rumbleslush of the machine, the spurt of soap water spiralling down midnight drains.

In the end, Dad made her go to swimming lessons. When we went to the pool, she did this trick the moment I blinked. She'd slide under the water and I'd lose her between the wobbly white legs and the rubber heads and the alien goggles.

Later, she would pop up at the far end of the pool like a fat mermaid, and scowl.

Funny joke, right. After all that, she could swim better than any of us. A Natural.

When I was ten I told my mother I would no longer take baths. It was dirty, I told her. I had to shower. She thought I was being a brat again, and I had to throw one of my epic screaming fits, piss myself so that I knew I had control, until Dad told her that letting me shower was better than letting me scream.

It wasn't that I hated bathing because of the filth, though that was part of it. Lying in warm water filled with flakes of skin and dirt and tiny fallen hairs and all the microscopic misery that attaches itself to human beings.

It was being lost in there, alone, disintegrating with my own debris. I was scared that one day I'd forget how to pull all my million selves back into one me, solid and real. It was better to lose myself in invisible pieces, sluiced away down the shower drain. I could hold my shape there, and just let the water wash out the parts of me I hated.

This is how to become water.

Take one sack of flesh bowed under the weight of its own unstoppable decay.

I learned how to become water before I was born. In Amnio. In water we are made, in water we will trust. I could dissolve and reform my bones, pull them together like sharpening splinters, stitch my molecules together and unpick them. I drifted between shapes. Growing.

When my mother's water broke, I had to claim my own space before there was nothing left of me.

I spent months curled into my new form, learning solidity. Vernix oiled away, sponged clean, skin revealed, hair black and flat, eyes puffed and swollen. I'd had a fight with the birth canal, that channel shaping my malleable flesh into form, squeezing my head firm, pounding out the air and the water, like a potter moulding clay. I only learned to become water again when my mother stopped sitting on the edge of the bath, watching me to make sure I wouldn't drown. I could lie under the warmth, listening to the boom and rattle of the pipes, the slow drip from the faulty tap and I could remember how to breathe water instead of air, and fill my lungs with a familiar warm salt. I could let go my bladder, and float in that familiar world of Amnio. It wasn't running away. It was running back.

Day by day I learned to dissolve.

Once, I walked into the bathroom while Claire was supposed to be having a bath. She was ten, I think, and I was sixteen and meant to be going out, tired of waiting and knocking and getting no response. She was a brat, a wild haired, sullen-eyed, bed-wetting, disappearing brat. And I was angry all over again with everything she was. So I shoved the door open, expecting to find Claire lolling in cooling water, her expression mulish.

There was no Claire.

There was only water, dark and strange and smoky with blood and hair.

I grew myself back after that, as quickly as I could I knitted myself together.

It had to stop.

It didn't.

Each slip was harder to come back from. My skin itched to

disappear, to fly away spark by spark to join the clouds and rivers, the sea and sweat and tears.

I know where my sister has gone. I can't say it, but I know it and it is why. Why I write her name in breathmist, and open my mouth to swallow the rain. Why I take long baths until the water around me is icy and my fingers and toes have shrivelled and pruned themselves numb. Why I don't change the stagnant water in my mother's flowers.

It's all right, Claire. We love you. Come back.

I fold my soul around Alison's daughter as she jumps in mud puddles under a sky dry from weeping. I settle in my mother's weakening bladder, run down her legs, I rinse the sadness from my sister's skin. From a cloudless sky I pull my molecules from mist so fine no man could see them.

I fall with the dusk on the waiting graves, and try to remember how to put myself together.

I'm fascinated by people who choose to disappear. Serein is the story of two sisters – the one who disappears and the one who is left behind – told in alternating points of view. My idea was that the sister who disappeared might want to come back but she can't. In this case, because she's become the rain.

Dreaming Monsters

We left Cacophony to gather dreams on the Long Road. It was decemberish and the light was fading, so the pilgrims were all wrapped up in constellations made out of wires and lights, and the sound of their plainsong moaned down the wide barren stones of the Long Road. We travelled behind them in a caravan drawn by three black manticores, their teeth pulled and their eyes put out. It was the easiest way to keep them docile.

Tania sat on the shoulders of the oldest manticore and guided her with a songwhip. My sister is no good at dreaming, but she knows animals and she can flay a man with her voice if she needs to. For the moment she was content to let the chanting pilgrims soothe the animals, their lulling sounds keeping the beasts to the track.

No one wants to wander off the Long Road, especially if they don't know their way around dreaming. There are things out there even I am afraid of, and I can swim a dream as fast as a little fish can flick through a burn. Things worse than the manticores and the dragons and unicorns that travellers normally use.

The gorgons in dreaming were dragon-limbed, like six-legged serpents, with the upper bodies of women, their round faces flat and empty, devoid of emotion. I had once seen one pulling a merchant caravan. Like all dreaming monsters on the Long Road, it had been blinded. The serpents that coiled about its face had not been, however, and they had watched me with their black glass eyes, tongues flickering as they tasted the air.

The gorgon had growled when I came too close, showing a row of splinter teeth. And it had spoken. Even the human-headed manticores never used human speech. "Fancy," the gorgon had said, in its thousand hisses. "Sweetmeat and dreamer, fancy. Dream-meat and sweeter. Fancy," before the driver had cuffed it with the rounded end of a long staff. Even after I had hurried back to my own caravan and to my grandmother, I'd felt its empty gaze on me.

"Janice," my mother said, soft and patient, her voice just rising over the click of her needles. She knitted memories, taking scraps of discarded clothing and tearing them into long thin strips which she knotted together and wound into rainbow-hued balls that she looped and slipped, looped and slipped as she stitched them into squares.

Her hands were worn smooth without a trace of a past or future. It came from working the memories deep into the warp and weft of the fabric, and making them into protection. The squares would all eventually be pieced together into blankets, and sold at Jarry market for good gold coin. It was how we made most of our money. "You're supposed to be sleeping."

"I am sleeping," I told her, and it was true enough; my eyes were closed. "It's just that my ears take longer to fall asleep than my eyes, and my brain longer still."

She clicked her tongue, and whispered numbers under breath, counting stitches. "We'll need you to go dreaming soon," she said. "A few more gloamings and we'll be in Jarry."

Dreaming was how we lived. My grandmother and I were the only ones in our family who could slip safe off the Long Road and into the slurry and flurry, and return in one piece, minds intact and bodies solid and whole. Most people who went dreaming lost themselves and turned to nothingness.

Most people don't come back.

We went there to collect the scraps my mother knitted into blankets. Clothes from before the dream-time, still warm from the people who had once worn them. They were always warm.

We gathered all kinds of things from the dreaming. Food, sometimes, though few people liked the taste of it; ashy and sour. The best-sellers used to be jewellery, though trade in that had thinned recently. Wine and spirits were the current market favourite, and Grandmother and I had built up a solid collection of dusty bottles that filled the crates in the caravan. They clinked softly, a sound lost under the wheels, and the plainchant, and the scritch-scratch-padsteps of the manticores.

Though there were no moon or stars here, and the sun nothing more than a distant orange-red glow, there was still the gloaming, when the heat dropped and the sun turned green and cold. The gloaming was the most dangerous time, especially if one was far from the cities and out on the Long Road. During gloaming, the priests sang louder and turned their constellations brighter. People stopped their caravans and hobbled their blinded monsters; their manticores and unicorns, their sphinxes and littling dragons. The monsters knew the gloaming was theirs. When the light faded the dreaming pressed closer, and the monsters howled for their lost home. The plainsong was meant as much to drown them out as anything else.

Tania slowed the manticores, and Mother sighed and set aside her knitting. From the back of the caravan I could hear Grandmother fussing with the pots and cleavers. The hiss of the gas sounded as the caravan drew to a halt. The rattle of wheels had been a constant background noise, and now it was gone, and the priests' voices rose higher.

From farther down the road, a dragon began to scream, and was answered by the whinnying shriek of a clutch of unicorns. Soon, the road would vibrate with the sound of their calls. Gloaming.

Our family set about the business of setting up camp: Tania fed the manticores chunks of dog-meat taken from the gas-run chest fridge bolted to the back of the caravan, my mother laid out the folding table and chairs right in the middle of the Long Road, and raised lanterns on poles. After they fed, Tania muzzled our manticores so that they wouldn't howl. She could do that because she was able to sing them calm, a neat trick to save yourself a few nasty scars, or dismemberment. Meanwhile, I worked side by side with Grandmother, washing the dishes while she ladled out the food she'd prepared. I breathed deep, the savoury and herbs of the rich meat, the clouds of dumplings bobbing and steaming. Grandmother had not just taught me to dream, but to cook too. We always worked as a team, compensating for the other, hardly even needing to talk.

Dreaming had made us strange, perhaps, and had left a gap in the family that Mother and Tania could never cross.

"Smells delicious." I slopped stew into bowls my gran had brought back from dreaming even before I was born, their pattern as familiar to me as the light-edged unreality of that other world only we could visit.

"On with you, girl," Grandmother said, but the words were affectionate as they were brusque, and I took the food out to the waiting table, where the others had already settled with their dreaming wine, the water we gathered from the occasional rains.

Around us, other road families were doing the same. Everyone set out extra bowls for the priests, because they were on pilgrimage to the church of Jarry, and part of their faith included poverty.

We were halfway through our meal when the priest approached our table. She wore her robe and constellations wrapped tight around her as though she were punishing herself for some half-forgotten sin, and she was tall and thin, with deep hooded eyes, statue-eyes, though hers were gloaming-blue, and not empty. Her eyes met mine, and something in them flickered, and was gone before I could catch it, like the last notes of a song only heard once.

Mother and Tania and I stood, though Grandmother carried on sucking the bones of her small chicken wing.

"Peace," said my mother, and gestured for the priest to take the empty seat we had left. The priest nodded in thanks. She looked weary, her feet ash-grey from slogging along the road, her face gaunt under her short curling hair. Her constellations flickered weakly – she'd need her batteries recharged soon, or she'd be deadspace before the reached Jarry. She didn't talk. After spending all day singing, I'd be surprised if she could, but it wasn't that. Apart from the plainsong, the pilgrims have all taken a vow of silence.

Ridiculous, perhaps, but priests are clowns of the sublime, just as we dreamers are the sublimest of clowns. She took her bowl of stew readily enough, and nodded gratefully.

"Well," said Grandmother, setting down the gnawed little bones onto her plate. "Come along, Janice-my-girl, it's time to dream." Grandmother doesn't have time for priests, just as they have little time for us. The Church has changed, become harsher towards dreamers, forgetting perhaps that we are their last link with the world as it was before.

The priest looked up curiously at the two of us, her gaze never leaving me as I curtseyed my thanks for the meal. Even as I walked to the caravan, trailing my tiny grandmother, it felt to me as though the priest's eyes were burning into my back like dropped coals.

Dreaming is done while still awake. We have a small curtained room in the one corner near the front of the caravan, where we can wash ourselves in purification and light a pipe to use as a dream-anchor. Grandmother and I both removed our clothes, folding them neatly. It was a ritual I had been repeating since I was old enough to walk. Before then, I would have to sleep in my gran's arms every night, so that she could keep me from drifting across without understanding, to become lost and invisible, a memory of a memory. Perhaps that is why my mother seems so resentful. Her mother stole her baby from her, though it was not her fault.

She was trying to save me. If she hadn't caught me that first time I fell into dream, I would have been simply another story told to scare new mothers – the baby gone in the morning, with nothing left in the crib but its swaddling clothes.

There were other stories of course; ones where the baby was gone, but something else was in its place. Changelings and nightmares. We don't talk of them.

We could take nothing with us from the road, from the world. The water in the washbowl was warmed and mother had set out clean towels for drying. Soon the two of us were ready – a wrinkled and bowed little grandmother who had taught me how to walk dreams, and me, her apprentice. Not a curse or a blessing to be able to walk dreams, but perhaps a bit of both, and in our family there was always at least one.

I took a last deep breath of salvia smoke before we stepped out of the purification room. Smoke came with us, tendrilling grey threads though the caravan space, filling it with the spicy taste that seemed to coat the back of my tongue. This is how we would find our way home. Grandmother used to tell me that when she was a child, her own grandmother told her of a time when the Church still allowed the hermits to use chant to call us back, but that the anchorites had all been destroyed when the antipopes went to war. Now the Church of Sinursula was powerless – little more than a cult – while the new regime had raised the Great Cathedral of Jarry, and we had to rely on the uncertain smoke. It made no difference to me – the smoke was all I'd ever known.

"Soon you'll be going in alone," said Grandmother.

"Not yet." I smiled at her and took her hand, soft and wrinkled as old paper, pushed open the door and we went down the steps together. Although we were naked as plucked hens, no one watched us. People knew better than to ogle. Most pretended to be discreetly busy with something else. Plainsong and howling followed us through the dark to the verge of the road, where this part of our world ended, and the dusk nothingness of the dreaming began. I took a little gasping breath like a swimmer about to duck underwater, and crossed over. The barrier between waking and dreaming popped like a soap bubble against my face.

Grandmother's hand tightened in mine and I looked to her. The Long Road and the caravans and the priests were gone. We were standing in a city street, the lamps shining yellow around us, and the stars distant pricks of light through the smog. The air here was thick and tasted like a rubbish tip. Not the kind of place where manticores and their sort would prowl, but gorgons liked cities, and they were smarter than the others. "Watch out," I said. "Snake-head country." My voice was a whisper and it still carried through the night. The dreamers here would never wake, but monsters never slept.

Grandmother was surveying the area. We had less than half an hour before the smoke anchoring us to the caravan would fade, and we'd need to work quickly. "Those apartments." She pointed up at a tall building like a temple of mirrors and glass, its edges flaming softly with dream-aura. "Be good pickings there." We didn't waste any more time, just marked the area where we had entered the dreaming, and moved. I was younger and faster, so I would take the higher levels. The doors were unlocked, and only the sentry was there to stop us. He was asleep where he stood, invisible to the waking eye. Only his uniform told me where he was – it was like a wrapping on a ghost. I ignored him.

"Dream safe," I said to Grandmother.

"Dream well," she replied. Another tradition older than both of us. I left her, and ran up the first and second flight of stairs and tried every lock until I came to one that turned under my hand.

In and out. Fast as a cat running from a wolfhound, that's how you needed to be in dreaming. Fast and quiet. The front room of the apartment was dark, the only light spilled in faintly from the street-lamps below. A set of pyjamas sat on an armchair, resting in front of a box humming with static. The person inside them was probably small and slight, from the looks of thing. A teenager, perhaps. I crept past the dreamer and headed through to the main bedroom, where two lumps under the duvet were all that showed who dreamed here. The dreamers never woke. They never move. For all we know they're already dead, or trapped in some endless ghost loop.

We can't see them, but we can touch them.

I don't. I've done it before, and settling my hands on nothingness and feeling the warmth of skin was unnatural. It made me feel like a thief, or a murderer. So I never took clothes or trinkets from the dreamers, though I know some do. Instead I ignored the dreamers, and made my way to the closet to grab a handful of the brightest clothes I could find. My mother liked bright colours – reds and yellows like flowers and suns. The fabric was warm. Even when they come straight from the hangers they feel warm, like they've just been stripped off.

You get over it.

With my bundle of clothes tucked under one arm, I made a quick dart into the kitchen, to raid their wine rack. Not every house has one, but it's worth it to look for a bottle here and there. Once we came dreaming right by a store filled with bottles of wine. That was a good haul, but we've never been that lucky since. I filled a shopping bag with as much wine as I could, then breathed deep. The salvia smoke was fading. Time to head back.

It was a good haul, and Grandmother would be pleased. The door clicked closed behind me, and the long shadows rippled as I made my way back down the hall and stairwell, to where we were supposed to meet. It seemed I'd been quicker than her, and I stood alone under the golden streetlight, in the whispering silence, watching the motionless guard at the entrance to the apartment building. At any moment, Grandmother should come though those glass doors, her own arms filled.

I waited.

Breathed deeply. The smell was going and I need to be able to follow it back. My heart began to beat faster and, despite my nakedness, a faint sheen of sweat beaded my back and brow. There are other reasons to get out of dreaming fast. A howl shot through the darkness, with that high human shriek so typical of a manticore. Another answered it. They hunt in small family packs, usually, but this lot sounded far away. Still, it was enough to make me breathe faster, shallower. Where in Jarry's Sweet Hell was my grandmother?

I shifted my weight, and willed myself not to look at my hands, my arms. I'd count out another minute. Sixty, but I was already growing weaker, could feel my heart slowing in my chest, my breaths coming farther apart. At thirty I tried to speak out loud, to call out for my missing grandmother, but there was no voice left in me.

At fourteen I looked down, saw the curl of the plastic handles of the shopping bag through my paling hand, and knew I couldn't wait any longer. With a shuddering gasp, I wrenched myself out of the pool of light, and breathed deep, gasping until I tasted salvia. Every movement felt slow and heavy, like wading through mud, and with each step the mud-feel thickened as dreaming got its claws into me. My heart would have been fluttering like the wings of a sunbird if it could have. There was no room in my head or my body for panic. Just a languorous urge to lie down, to give in.

To sleep.

It wasn't the smoke that saved me and pulled me back home. It was a single voice, raised in the language of waking. Like a needle, it caught the thread of me and led me through the silken dreams and back to the Long Road. City lights popped bright, faded, and I found myself on dusty stone, the caravan's flags flapping and cracking in a dismal wind, face to face with the shabby thin priest of Jarry, her cold clear voice still cutting through the rising storm and the angry cries of the monsters.

"Thank you," I said, when my words filled me up again like a clear water spring breaking through thick mud.

The priest fell silent and bowed her head.

Mother and Tania only looked past me, where there was no Grandmother.

"I – I'm sorry." Though I had no idea what I was apologising for. For leaving? For doing what I had been trained to do? I waited longer than I should have. And now she was gone, part of dreaming, a ghostling thing.

I began to shiver and cry. I dropped my precious haul, and one of the bottles smashed, the sound of shattering glass mocking what I had lost. My body folded up on itself and I collapsed in the dust, the wind ripping at my hair, lashing my skin raw. It was the priest who covered me with a robe starred in flickering light.

We reached Jarry before decemberish muddled into janrish. The city was garlanded with lamps in every colour, and the Great Cathedral with its rosy window bled holy light out to the blue-black sky. I was walking ahead of the caravan, leaning closer to the priest, her body like an anchor to replace the one I had lost.

I had not gone dreaming since Grandmother's loss, and my mother had used up all the clothes I'd brought back. She spent the days tearing them into strips, then knit knit knit. The days were filled with the hollow snicking of her needles.

Tania didn't talk to me. Wouldn't talk to me. Every time I drew near her she would turn her face away, like I was a disease walking. And I could barely talk to mother, not when she wore a veil of tears and counted stitches over and over in a running mumble.

Instead, I talked to the priest. At least I knew she wasn't speaking to me because of her vows, and not because she hated me.

I walked with her, deep in the ranks of the singing priests, and let their chant keep me afloat. "It wasn't on purpose," I told her the first gloaming after, the first one without my grandmother. "I would never have chosen to leave her there. These things happen."

I told her this over and over, as if by repeating it I could cast some kind of spell to draw my grandmother back, to let her know that I had not forgotten her. And when I cried, my priest would nod, and hand me a square of linen to wipe my eyes. She would stroke my hair and hold me, while never missing a note in the song. In return, I charged her batteries from our windergig, and she shone bright as a jesus star the closer we drew to Jarry. Even the manticores seemed struck dumb by her glow, their howls stoppered.

She told me her name. Wrote it down for me with a finger drawn through dust. A tiny violation of her vows. Ebba, I would whisper when I was alone in my bed, staring at the birds Grandmother had painted on the ceiling. I began to think she was holier than the statues of the marys in Sinursula. Kinder, certainly. And isn't it kindness and gentleness and mercy the bear-girls preach?

When we saw the lights of Jarry, I clung to Ebba, begged her not to leave me, to stay by my side no matter what. There were Wakeford Houses in Jarry, where all manner of dreamers gathered. And some of them had Doorwaymen where I could go to find a way to search out my grandmother, but I could tell no one this, especially not my family – who would not have understood the risk – nor my priest, who would not have agreed.

Ebba looked uncertain, but she sighed and nodded, and in my chest hope kindled, and something else. What is comfort, and silence, and a warm and sympathetic body, if not a kind of love? I took her hand and squeezed it tight. It was warm and firm, and nothing like my grandmother's, but I held it fast anyway, because I wanted to, because to let go would have sent a message I did not want to send to my priest. My Ebba. I hoped she understood.

"You will have to sell the wine alone," my mother told me. Normally I went with Grandmother, and watched her haggle and reason with the priests and the bear-girls, but now the job was mine. I shivered, and glanced at Ebba, a wordless question, and she nodded in answer.

She came with me to sell the dreaming wine for communion to the sour speechless men at the Cathedral, and then to the bear-girls at Sinursula's. They looked at her from under their furs and frowned and said nothing. All around me was silence and I could understand no one's unwords. At least with Grandmother there had always been chatter and talk, and Tania would sing and the monsters would wail. I felt like a ghostling myself, drifting further and further away from my family. My heart went small in my chest, and ached with the hurt of losing her. Not for long, I told myself, and swallowed back my tears.

When I spoke to Ebba, my voice was steady, betraying nothing. "Have you been to Jarry before?"

Ebba shook her head. We'd packed away her constellations – it was considered bad form to wear them in Jarry itself – and I'd loaned her one of my tunics so she wouldn't have to worry about people wondering why a priest was travelling about with a sketchy dreamer, a sinner like myself. It was a little short on her, seeing as how she was a long-shanked thing, with a serious long face to match, but it changed her. If not for the silence, I would think her any Long Road caravaner trading in flotsam and jetsam. She'd not gone with the other pilgrims to the Great Cathedral, and I wondered why.

"The market's what we're mostly here for. You're not, of course, but there's more to the city than the Cathedral, believe it or not." I would talk to fill up her voicelessness. I took her hand, and she let me. "The best places, though, are the ones only the dreamers know. I'll take you to them." Strictly speaking, I shouldn't have let a regular person into one of the Wakeford Houses, but though the Church loves us only a little, I wanted to trust her. More than that, I needed her, and what she could do for me.

The House I was looking for was close to the central Jarry market, at the end of a knot of alleyways. It was the part of town where people looked strangely at two women walking alone, and our feet moved faster under their stares. It was the only House I knew of that had a mapkeeper, and a reputation for illegal trade. Perhaps not the best place to bring a priest.

Die Eend en Esel was burrowed downstairs beneath a traveller's inn, and the sunken network of rooms was lit in reds and blues, and filled with bits and things plucked from dreaming. It was a jackdaw's nest, a viper's den, a smoky hole for waking dreamers to meet and drink oneiric wine, to boast and warn, trade and piece together the imperfect maps that make up the world we did not understand.

The people here knew me; by the smell of my skin, by the ripples I had left behind in the dreaming, by the pattern of my walk. "Alia's apprentice," said the barkeep, her black hair bound up in ribbons woven in red webs. "Janet."

"Janice."

"And where's Alia, then. Too good for the likes of us?" She reached down to pour a streamer of black-red wine into a glass. "Who's your friend?"

"Ebba," I said. I ignored the question about Grandmother. Better to say nothing than to lie.

"You'll be drinking?"

Ebba nodded carelessly as though she were born to taverns like this one and had sipped on dreaming wine all her life. Once we had our glasses, I paid, and downed mine for courage. It tasted like black tar and the peculiar dustiness of dreaming. Ebba copied me, and our glasses kissed the counter.

We pushed through the strangeling crowd to the very back rooms, where the doors were always locked, and only the right words would open them.

I rapped softly at the third door, then whispered low. My grandmother taught me these words, always, I suppose, thinking I would never have to use them. Ebba watched me with a curious frown, then followed me in when the door opened.

The tiny room was thick with salvia smoke and panelled in bronze mirrors. A small man with a round face half-hidden under a hat like the bent pipe of a stove sat in the only chair in the room, and behind him rose a patterned wardrobe, carved and painted with angels. Most of them were worn away, and the wood was cracked from lack of care. But it pulsed. Powerful. My head began to ache in time with it, right through the roots of my teeth.

"And what have we here?" said the man. His voice was choked up, thick with the smoke. "Two misfits."

"You're the Doorwayman," I answered. "And I need you to get me to a specific place in dreaming. Can you do that or not?" I pretended a casual certainty I did not feel, and clenched my teeth against the rattling power coming from the carved wardrobe.

He narrowed his eyes, smiled, and considered. He didn't disguise the way he stared us up and down, though he said nothing, perhaps weighing what he could get out of us. Ebba caught my sleeve just below the elbow, as though she wanted to drag me back from a precipice.

"And she's going to be your anchorite." He nodded at Ebba. "I can't make promises that even a priest will bring you back."

"How do you –?" He wouldn't let us leave this room alive if he thought Ebba were really a priest. A fence I'd climb when we reached it. For now, I would tackle each problem as it came to me. I shook my head. Carefully, I described the area where I'd lost Grandmother, though I didn't mention her once. Ebba's face turned ashen, and she twisted my sleeve.

I ignored her. "Can you get me to the right spot?"

The man stood, his bent top-hat crooking even further. "I know the place, and I can get you there." His teeth gleamed.

"How much?" This is the art my family would not understand. A Doorwayman is a robber, a thief – he controls the only maps we have of dreaming, and the only doorways that lead to specific places. For this, he can charge what he likes, and what he likes is never easy, or cheap.

"A head full of snake's teeth," he said, and my stomach filled with heavy pebbles, like a sack meant for drowning.

"I –" Can't. I wanted to say, but I had to. I could take no weapons with me into dreaming, but that didn't mean I wouldn't be able to find something there. I was fast and quiet like my gran had trained me to be, and if it took a gorgon's head to get me there and back again to save her, I'd do it. I faced Ebba, and put one hand over hers where it clutched at my sleeve. "I know I wasn't entirely honest with you," I whispered quickly. "But please, do this for me. One thing, be my hold so I can have more time. Sing my name and bring me back." The salvia smoke would give me only a half hour at best, before dreams claimed me, but if Ebba could anchor me home, I should be safe for longer. Safe enough to walk straight into a gorgon's pit? Perhaps not, but it gave me time and I could think of nothing else. I wasn't ready to lose my grandmother.

And if I failed and died, so what? What was there for me to come back to here? I was one half of a dreaming pair, and lost.

When Ebba spoke to me for the first time, her voice was nothing like the high sweet sound of her singing. If I had never heard her chant before, I would have thought them the voices of two different people. "It is not allowed," she said, a blunt saw on greenwood.

"Neither is this." I tightened my hand on hers, feeling the sweat-damp skin, the thrum of her pulse. We were close enough that I could smell her under the choking salvia – a combination of sweetmusk and road dust, incense and sour wine. "You should never have spoken to me. And I act with good cause. You know that."

"Come now, ladies. Time is short."

I glanced at the wardrobe full of angels, opened now to a dizzy mist that sucked at my skin. The man was calibrating a piece of chalk on a movable metal arm, and marking a spot on a map pasted on the interior of one of the doors. The corners of the map were peeled up, ragged edged. I could understand nothing of the names and markings, but the Doorwayman nodded and clucked to himself in satisfaction. It was illegal to keep maps of dreaming, to try control it as though it were simply another part of our world. While his price was high, he could be burned as a heretic if the Church knew what he could do – what he did.

The opening pulled at me. "Please. Help me. Like your godman helped others."

Ebba let go my sleeve and twisted her hand free of mine. "An hour," she said.

My heart lifted. It would have to be enough. "Thank you." I would find some way of paying her back, for making her break her vows. I've never had time for the Church and their two-faced view on dreaming – a sin, they said, while their stewards bought oneiric wine from us so they could see the face of god, but it hurt to think I had forced Ebba to break her vows. I might have no care for the Church, but she did. Not understanding her faith gave me no right to bruise it, to twist it to my own needs.

"I'll give you a warning when you have a quarter hour left," she told me. She touched my face before I turned away, a brush brief and slight.

"Thank you." This time it hurt to say, the crystalline realisation that I wanted more than anything to come back. With my grandmother, with the gorgon head. I did not want to die, to not see Ebba again. I stripped the guilt off me, peeling it away with each piece of clothing. I made myself hard and bright and clean-of-thought as a star. In and out. Fast and quiet. Find, kill, save.

Find, kill, save.

Apologies I'd have time for later. I would, I told myself. Because I was coming back.

The night was misted, and the street lamps were orbs of clouded yellow light that floated like a twin row of angels snaking into the distance. I sniffed, tried to orient myself. Was this where Grandmother and I had come? It took a moment before I made out the glass-panelled building where I'd made my run. It was farther away this time. I breathed deep, and listened to the distant singing of Ebba coming through the dark. My name, caught in among the petal-words of the chant like a small black thorn. It hooked at me and I smiled grimly.

There was no chance I'd see my grandmother now, not when she'd been in dreaming so long. She'd be ghosted like the rest of them, sleeping and silent, and in her case – naked. But I would find her, I'd promised this to myself. To her. She had to be near the building we'd raided. She'd taken the first floor. Already that limited the area I had to search.

With Ebba's song hooked into my heart, I twisted a long thin branch down from a roadside tree, and began to use it to brush the road and grounds before me in a wide arc. I'd never been the methodical type, but this time I concentrated, mapping out the area square by square, covering every inch. It was painstakingly slow.

An hour, Ebba had said. My skin grew clammy, sweat running down my brow as I worked. The branch swept this way and that, as though I were trying to divine water from dry earth. Not once did it come across any invisible obstacle. How long had I been searching?

Impossible to tell. Ebba had agreed to give me a fifteen-minute warning but I hadn't heard it. Had I missed it? I paused. I was in the stairwell now, going over each step carefully. Around me the song echoed softly, chiming like bells.

Another sound rumbled below it, just on the edge of hearing. I stood still, my heart too loud, blood thudding and whooshing in my eardrums. I pressed myself back against the wall, tried to slow my breathing. The branch hung limp in my right hand.

A soft tic tic tic pause tic pause tic tic. A hiss and a rattle. Behind my head and back, the cold smooth wall of the stairwell felt like ice. My sweat chilled against the paint. Plainsong and claws on concrete.

The branch in my hand vibrated gently, as though moved by a gentle breeze. Close your eyes. Serpent-head. I remembered the empty stare of the gorgon I had seen so many years ago. Like all monsters it had been blinded, but with gorgons there was good cause. Their stare freezes you in your tracks, makes it easier to tear its prey apart.

And the voice. It had spoken like a human, but with an underlying mesmerising hiss that had made me lose my breath, had addled my thoughts.

"Dreammeat," hissed the stairwell gorgon from the floor below me, and my stomach iced up, my blood thickening in my veins. I had no weapon, no mirror, nowhere to run.

I remembered the teeth of the other. Needle sharp.

Tic.

"Fancy," said this monster. "My sister's fancy." The serpents hissed and rattled, and the plainsong drifted out of hearing. Around me the shadows had deepened. I could wait here, and die, or take my chance and run. I looked down at my trembling hand. Through the skin, I could see blue rivers of veins, the pale gleam of bone. I could see the faint outline of the whip-thin branch.

Too late. I had missed Ebba's warning, my hour had ended.

Soon, I would be gone, and after that... I had no idea. How long before I fell asleep and became one of the dreamers, curled up where I had fallen, oblivious to all around me? I dropped the branch and it landed with a thin sound that echoed around and down the stairs.

Below, the gorgon hissed. "Sweetling, ghostling, dreamthing," it said, and hissed again. Laughter, I realised. And then I ran.

Up, because there was nowhere else to go. Soon the slow-as-mud feeling would catch up with me. It would have made more sense to simply lie down and wait for sleep, for nothing, but even at the end of it all, I couldn't. Some human thing in me kicked and bit and wanted to live. And so I ran.

The gorgon gave chase, winding along like an overgrown snake on taloned-legs, always speaking. The voice was meant to mesmerise, to still its prey and make for an easy kill. But I have lived all my life around the plainsong of the priests, around the chants of the bear-girls, and in my head, I began to sing, to drown out the sound of the gorgon's "Fancy, fancy, fancy, sweetmeat, dreamling. Lingerling."

The song gave me courage, lent my feet fleetness; I turned down a corridor, another, another, until I reached another set of glass doors – almost ran into them, if it hadn't been for the dull red strip at waist-height, and the words FIRE ESCAPE. I glanced back, just enough to see the deeper shadow of the gorgon flickering on the wall.

"Lingerling," it said. "Fingerling."

The only light here came from the high windows at the top of the passage walls, and they let in barely more than a dimming candle-glow. Not enough for what I needed. There had to be a light switch for the hallway somewhere. Desperate, my breath coming in wretched gasps, I scanned the dark-draped shadows. I kept my back to the gorgon, terrified that at any moment it would pounce, that teeth like broken razors would shred down my spine, that I would die in agony as it chewed open my belly and pulled out the ribbons of my entrails. With my voice shaking, I spoke to the monster at my back. "Fingerling, smallthing, dreamersweet."

The gorgon paused, the tic of its talons suddenly silent. All I could hear now was the dry rasp of scales at the serpents twined over each other, their questioning hisses.

"Sweetmeat, wellmet, sistermet," I continued, hoping its confusion at prey that talked back would last a little longer. There. A light switch, high to the right. How long would it take me to reach it, and then open the fire door? If it was even unlocked. I had no way of knowing. I suppose if Ebba had been with me she would have suggested I pray, but I had no time for Jarry gods and bear-girls.

"Sister...." hissed the gorgon. It shook its head and the snakes rattled and quivered.

No more time to waste on thinking. I lunged for the light, and as the hallway exploded in brightness the gorgon leapt too, just catching my shoulder with its teeth. The pain was worse than burning, worse than the time I'd spilled hot oil across my knee. It was similar, in its way, but icy cold, and I was certain that it had cut through my whole arm, that if I turned to look I would see nothing there but meat and bone and blood.

I didn't look. Left-handed, I pushed at the bar on the fire escape, and the door swung open, and all around us the alarms began to scream. With the sound vibrating in my head, I slammed my back against the door, shutting it against the thud of the gorgon.

The clanging of the alarm echoed inside my skull, adding to the fierce pain in my right shoulder. But there was no further attack. After that first thud, the gorgon had gone still. I tipped my head back against the glass, and gently reached around to touch my arm. Where I hoped my arm would be. Warm flesh. I sobbed in relief, and finally let myself look. The bite had torn the muscle through the bone, and a flap of skin hung down. I'd need stitches. Lots of them. I thought of my mother sewing the squares of the dreamer's rainbow-hued blankets together, and the tears ran salt-ticklish down my face, into my mouth.

I wasn't going back. Slowly, the world already turning sluggish around me, I looked back at the gorgon. It was stone-still, illuminated under the white strip lighting, every detail clear. Caught by its own reflection in the glass door.

A hollow victory.

And then I heard it, far-away and faint as a hope.

Ebba's song, plainchant to pull me home, to hook under my skin, to keep me safe. Carefully and slowly, with one hand clamped to my shoulder, holding the wound closed, I cut the gorgon's head free with one of its own broken teeth. And with my useless trophy, I followed the song through dreaming back to Jarry, to Die Eend en Esel.

All things have their end, my grandmother once told me. She had hers, and if there had to be an ending more fitting for a waking dreamer than to fall into endless invisible sleep then I cannot think of one.

We are on the Long Road, from Jarry to Mestling, avrilish or thereabouts, by the fluid calendar of the priests. They are handing out boiled cockatrice eggs. Even Ebba doesn't know why.

"Tradition," she says, and undresses me, her fingers long and thin, warm and sweet, careful across the stiff scars on my shoulder. She folds each piece of clothing neatly before laying it across the back of the little seat where she will wait for me. She does not dream with me, but she holds me home each night, and sings me safe again.

Another short based on a novel-verse. I have a terrible habit of starting a story, getting lost in the world and never finishing the novel, but writing a multitude of shorts set in the same universe instead. This is the world of Mundus, of Jarry and the magic cities. It's a world concurrent to ours where angels steal poets, and dreamers slip through time to steal the flotsam and jetsam of human existence.

Golden Wing, Silver Eye

It is winter in Pal-em-Rasha and all the roosters have been strangled. We are in mourning. The prince was born white and strange, his dead sister clinging to his heel, and since then three weeks have passed without cock-crow.

People work with their heads bowed and their lips pinched. In the markets – normally ringing with calls and shouts and trades – money falls from palm to palm in muffled offerings. Even the People of the Dogs wrap the hooves of their shaggy red oxen with rags when they come down to the city from their mountain homes. Peasants chase the monkeys away from the orange groves and the tamarind trees, and the leaves hang dry and limp. The little brown doves do not heed the king's order for silence, and they line the buildings, chuckling at each other in low coos, taking turns to steal the fallen rice from between the road stones.

Our city is divided like a lotus, each petal some stronghold of trade or class. My Bee lives in the cogworker's district on Iron Ox road in her father's house. She has no memory of him. Like many men, he has fallen to war. There is only her and her mother, both pretending that this house they run, that they inhabit like snails inside a shell, belongs to them. They eke out his small fortune, watching it dwindle with every passing day.

Her mother climbs the stairs to the loft where Bee has her workshop, and I follow dutifully. I am not permitted to serve food these days. It pains me to see Old Mother struggling to carry the heavy tray up the narrow staircase and know that I am forbidden to help her. She pants as she manoeuvres the tray into the crook of one arm so that she can swing the door open.

Bee waves her mother away as the old woman clears a space on the clutter-strewn desk for the tea tray. "Kavi," Bee says without looking up at me. Her voice is low. Even in our own homes we speak in whispers, scared of offending the dead. Bee is at work on one of her creatures, its innards spread out across her work table: minute shining cogs and coiled wires fine as the tongue of a butterfly. Her eyeglass is strapped in place with leather bands, flattening her dark hair against her skull, and she looks like a drowned monster hunched over an open treasure chest.

I wait respectfully for Old Mother to leave before I answer. "What is it, my little bee?" The fragrant red sweetness of the tea lifts some of the oppressive funk of the dimly lit room. Even with all the shutters open wide, there is not enough light. The skies are weeping too, cold and bitter with dry snow.

The queen is dead, her children monsters or ghouls.

"I'll need new lenses," Bee tells me. "This one, even on its highest setting..." she pauses to unbuckle straps and pull the offending thing from her face. "It's not good enough." She takes the tea, sips, sighs. "It's simply not up to the kind of work I want to do."

The city of Pal-em-Rasha is famous from the high mountains to the bay of Utt Dih for its clockwork beasts. The temple mages from the mountains may sneer and call our people toymakers, but that only shows how scared they are of what we could do. The toymakers are the little gods building horses of bone and wood and metal for princes to ride into battle and birds to take messages, beetles to watch from the walls. Not all their creatures are simple cog and gear contraptions, wound to life with a key. The very best toymakers have also graduated from the floating university.

They are artists and metalworkers and magicians, skilled and powerful. My Bee builds creatures from shining metal and breathes life into them. She has made fine work. Not the finest, perhaps, but she did her time in the university, and her skills are much in demand. Just last month, she completed an order for a hair ornament for a prince merchant's wife. A moth made of silver, delicate as a live creature. After she'd breathed her soul into its metal heart, I pinned it to her own hair. We stood together in front of the bronze mirror her father had brought back more than twenty years ago from some borderland skirmish. Her reflection was bronzed as the mirror. The moth stirred its grey wings softly, shimmering against the black coils of her hair. I stood at her shoulder. Already, I was too pale and unhealthy against her brightness. She'd smiled in satisfaction, and I'd carefully caught the moth and boxed and wrapped it.

Now, she is working on something grander. My Bee is done with crawling things, small mechanical lives.

While she leans back in her chair and sips at her tea and nibbles on her mother's little coconut pastries, I pick up a feather from the open drawer in her beast-box. She spent many nights perfecting each one. There are flight feathers of heavy gold and thousands of down feathers no bigger than a baby's pinkie nail, each one made of metal filaments. The one I hold is from the wing, heavier than a real feather, of course, but otherwise almost identical.

My Bee is a master. One day, soon I think, they will know her name in the palace tower. She will be richer than the merchant princes who buy her art now. She will teach kings the meaning of life.

"You'll need to go down to the Oculary and buy me something better, higher magnification," she says. "I don't have the time now to go myself."

I'm her servant, true, but I am more than that, and I frown at her in wounded annoyance.

She catches my look and runs one hand through her hair. "Sorry, love." Her smile is tired, these long nights eating away at her brightness. "Please," she adds, almost as an afterthought.

It's not always easy: love. Especially when you love someone caught in their own genius, like a child trapped in a never-ending dream. Sometimes, they forget we are out here. Sometimes, they forget everything.

I nod. I will leave Old Mother a note telling her what Bee needs, and she can send one of the delivery boys out to collect it with the household orders. "Magnification?" I ask, carefully writing Bee's words down. I can still do this, at least. The quill-beast responds to my touch, clattering as it reacts to the pressure of my finger, the lightest brush. Bee made this one for me, back when we first fell in love.

We passed our hearts across doorways, secret and nervous. She, the treasured only child, burdened with talent and an expensive education, and I, a women's maid, burdened with hairbrushes and pins and pots of shadows. I had every excuse to touch her, and I took them all. These days she has no time for preening, and I drift through the house, neither one thing nor the other.

The rooster takes shape, day by day. First the skeleton, in gleaming bronze, its skull polished under the floating gas lamps Bee has gathered in the corners of the pitched roof. Then, as the hours pass and I watch, quiet from my cushion, the muscles and sinews of cogs and wires. At the end of every night, Bee folds her tools back into velvet, sighs and taps the creature, and sets it bobbing and pecking. The eyeless skull bowing to her.

"Why a rooster?" I ask her. I've enjoyed this time without the pre-dawn shrieking of the backyard barons.

She shrugs. "They are handsome, gold and green, crests and wattles like new-spilled blood, dragon eyes and claws. What's not to like?"

Because, I say inside my head, because then the spell will be broken, and I will have to go. I'm not the only one to have enjoyed this brief reprieve. We pass on the streets and nod to each other in unspoken acknowledgement. We watch the city hens with their trains of new-hatched chicks and wait for these little suns to grow feathers instead of fluff and brash voices instead of peeps. Some of them will grow spurs and proud tails, will crow the day awake.

And then we will leave.

The rooster's eyes lie on a work cloth darkened with metal dust. They look like beads strung on black wires. Bee has made them silver grey to stand out against the golden feathers. I watch them, and they watch me in return.

"Make something else." At her elbow is a glass bowl of leg scales made of electrum. I stir them with one finger as I talk, not looking at her face. "There are jungle crows in the south that have feathers of gold – you would only have to make a few small changes."

"The queen's standard was a rooster," she snaps.

"You think he will care?"

Bee stands in a huff, throwing a fallen loop of her silk wrap back over her shoulder. "Jealous, Kavi, because you have no art? Or scared that success will ruin what we have?" She dashes one hand across her eyes as though flicking away a lazy fly. "I'm doing this for us – if I can get a royal patronage, we can buy our own home, go anywhere we like. We can pay for the finest doctors and do as we will."

She's bitter because she's tired. She forgets because it's easier that way.

I say nothing. The rooster grins at me with its metal beak.

"Sorry," Bee says. "I don't mean to be so sharp. It's been a long day." She holds her arms open to embrace me. Her apologies always were as quick and raw as her attacks.

I step out of reach and slip past her.

Old Mother is waiting for me on the stairs.

We stop across from each other. Her wrinkled face, cross-hatched with sadness and fear for her daughter, peers up at me. I try to keep my own face a mask to hide my guilt. Guilt? *What have I to be guilty for?* I ask myself as I wait for Old Mother to speak.

"You should go," she says.

My answer catches in my throat, rust and broken edges.

"The longer you stay, the worse she gets," Bee's mother says, and the tears wash through the tiny valleys that map her cheeks. "You are driving her mad. You are hurting Bijri, and I do not think you want that."

I know, I want to say. But it's not me who chose to kill every rooster in the city. Perhaps, even now, the king sits in his high tower, in the Pistil of Pal-em-Rasha, holding his queen's cold hand and praying for miracles. I nod at her instead. I have heard, I have understood.

I wander into the little room that used to be mine when I was still just a servant. It's unoccupied, and I lie down on the narrow bed. It is colder and harder and meaner than Bee's, but it doesn't feel right to go and lie there now.

Through the wooden walls, the voices drift. Old Mother, coaxing Bee to come with her to a friend, to take in some fresh air and clear her head. Bee argues, but eventually she gives in, and their feet patter away, down hallways and staircases.

Alone in the house, except for the maid and cook who avoid me anyway, I take the opportunity to go into Bee's loft. The gas lamps are dead, but thin winter light still bathes the room enough that I can see. Bee must have been tired – she bowed to her mother's wishes. Far more telling: she left her tools out on the work bench, not rolled up in their velvet and put gently to bed like fragile children. She was working on the eyes again. Near them lies the clockwork heart, a bright ticker waiting for winding.

Childish temper, fear, anger. I don't know what it is that drives me, but I flick those watching eyes from the bench, and they rattle and bounce, lost to the wooden floorboards and the dark corners. I press one finger through the mechanics of the heart, upsetting the delicate balance of cog and wheel.

This will hurt her more, I realise. Not because I've broken a trinket, but because it will only make the leaving harder. I search the floorboards until my skirt and hands are streaked with dust. When I find the eyes, I put them back carefully next to the broken heart. That at least, I know Bee can fix. I leave the destruction and go hide in my old room. It is familiar-strange, a place I only came back to when I hurt, when I didn't want to distract Bee with my pain. It's hard to cry, but I find myself dampening the sun-bleached bedding with my faint tears.

"Found you," Bee says, waking me, her voice bright again. It seems the walk has done her good. "What are you doing here?" She lies down next to me on the servant's bed, gently shoving so that I will make room for her. We fold each other in our arms. We kiss and sing the song that only those who love know, that sweet low song.

"I was just thinking," I say when I have air again to speak.

"Don't," she commands. "It's made you miserable, whatever it was you were thinking about." She kisses me again, her lips warm, her tongue soft. She has eaten honeyed figs and drunk imported tea from the Ten Thousand Island Heaven Empire. "Never leave me," she says between kisses. "I know I'm a pain, but you make me human," she says between touches. "You are my right eye, my right hand –"

"Shh," I tell her.

"My right ventricle, my right foot, my right big toe –"

I quiet her with my mouth.

The rooster is almost done. The gas lamps are turned low, and the beast stands regal on the table. The feathers are soft gold, warm and welcoming. The tail curves high, black and green, each filament enamelled. It is a thing on the scalpel-edge of living. I look to the open windows where the darkness is still looped with stars. Outside, the birds have not yet woken, but they stir in their dreams of rice and grain.

"So?" Bee spreads her hands and looks to me. Under the arrogance is her fear. Am I good enough, or have I wasted my time, my money, have I deluded myself, tell me, tell me, tell me that my work is sweeter than palm sugar, more precious than salt. Please tell me. "What do you think?"

"It is very beautiful."

She sniffs. "Of course," but she winks after she says it and smiles, shy as a child.

"When will you present it to the king?" I lean forward from my seat and touch its beak. It shivers gently.

"Tomorrow," Bee says, and before I breathe deep at my momentary stay, she continues, "but first I need to make sure it will work."

I tuck my hands back in my lap, and the bangles she gave me as marriage gifts clatter softly.

"Pray for me, Kavi. Pray to your funny little house gods." But she doesn't wait for me to say yes or no, so eager. She's a child showing off, caught up in the joy of her creation. Bee bows her head, her eyes closed. She looks like a temple reverent, her dark lashes spider leg shadows on hollow sockets, her ringlet hair unbrushed for days. Like all students of the floating university, the first thing she ever learned was stillness, to tame her breath, to use it to call up power from the earth and channel it. Her breath is her magic, machinery her art. The air changes as the magic builds, gathering in her belly. Minutes pass as she charges her breaths, pulling energy from the lifewells that track below the skin of the world. Before, I wasn't attuned to these currents of power, but now I can feel them. I can see ribbons of light. The dark hair on my arms stands up, and a million spiders dance out a strange new song against my skin.

The breath moves from body to body. From warm lips to cold bright beak, and like paper catching fire, the energy crackles along every wire and cog, turns the dead heart into a lightning pulse. The rooster opens one dragon eye on me.

Oh, enemy.

There is still time before dawn, before daybreak, but my lover's art has no care. It throws back its gleaming head, heavy feathers flushed with warmth and magic.

First crow.

The sound is harsh and over-loud in the loft, and it tears the anchor of my heart, uproots me.

"Kavi!" Bee says, cheeks and eyes shining. "Look! Oh, Kavi, our fortunes are made." She turns away from her monster to catch my hands and draw me to my feet, to spin me around in a tight dance. She is hot and breathless, and her kiss tastes like bitter tea and too little sleep and funerary coins. "Oh, love, you're so cold," she says when she draws back from me, brow crinkling in concern. "You've been so patient with me, and I've been ignoring you." She holds me tight, drawing me close to her until I can pretend her heartbeat is mine.

Second crow.

My feet disappear first. Bee cannot see them, hidden under my long skirt of red ochre. My legs and hips fade, and all that is left is painstaking embroidery and rustling linen. I grow light.

"Are we still fighting?" she asks me, her breath damp against my ear, and I will her magic into me. If I were made of cogs and wires, she could make me dance again.

"You forgot," I whisper back, but the rooster has thrown back his sharp head, opened wide his savage beak. He crows again and there is no more time left.

Three crows to call the dead home.

We leave Pal-em-Rasha in a sea of misting grey, thick as dreams. The shades that have spent the weeks since the king's command in a hell of waiting. The pull rushes us, whistling hard in our ears, dragging us willing or no. I force myself to turn my head and look back down at the house where I died alone, retching up blood in a servant's room so that my lover would not see.

Bee dances in her loft, the empty pleated skirt and tunic top held crumpled in her arms. Her tears fall bright as feathers. On the workbench, the golden rooster struts and calls.

Another world, another short. I'm proud to say this novel I did actually finish, so there's that. "Golden Wing, Silver Eye" is about love and clockwork, magic and ghosts. It was originally written for a steampunk anthology, but I tend to find the Victoriana Steampunk thing a bit overdone, so I went in a very different direction.

I'm Only Going Over

There are a million of them, flicking between worlds faster than grasshoppers, the whine of their wings cicada summers, white scythes sighing.

I caught one, once. Or it caught me.

We are at a party. Teen drama of stupid petty fights that happen under electric light, in sterilized bathrooms and modern kitchens, stealing vodka from a liquor cabinet, topping up the bottles with water. Cheap crackling wine bought from under the counter at the local corner shop. She's watching us and talking to no one. Lonely, maybe. I thought she was just some friend of a friend of a friend's. No one gatecrashes lame parties like this. Louise had thrown it – telling her mom she's inviting a few friends 'round, and she's so big-eyed and neat and she'd never be like that, oh no, and of course her parents believe her.

So here we all are, half drunk on watered-down spirits and being seventeen. Some best of Pandora station is playing and it is bland as shit. I've been watching the girl from the other room, kinda falling in not-love but hey, I wanna know your name and chase your smile through the dark.

She reminds me of my childhood, when the nothings would come sit with me when I hid in the little alleyway on the side of the apartment, and tell me that it would get better. It had for them, they said. I just had to wait until the time was right. And then I grew up, and I stopped inventing imaginary saviours. Now I look for the other people who don't fit in, and we have a five-minute connection. Or a one minute, or whatever. At least they're real, and we both know no one's ever going to save us.

She's one of us, dragged here to a stranger's house by someone who has already deserted her. We could be soul mates.

Russell is well on his way to falling-down drunk, making out with some girl he'll mock in the morning. Tracy, looks like. He hates Tracy. He's just doing this to make Janine jealous. It's all so bloody pathetic. I look away from the bodies on the couches, from the middle-class floor lamps with their middle-class fringes, back to the girl on her own. I walk over, proud that I don't stumble or trip. I am completely cool.

The friend of a friend of a friend is sitting on the kitchen counter, black hair falling over her face, head bowed, feet swinging. She's wearing a long scarlet coat in some fluttery material that drapes and flows as she moves. She's got a cigarette thin as a matchstick in one hand, but I never see her smoke it. It doesn't smell right. Not like weed either, too dry and clean. The smoke veils her hand, twisting about itself, dragons chasing their own tails.

"Hey," I say, because I am suave as fuck. I am drunk on lethe water and running away. I have bruises across my ribs and a black mark on my heart. This gives me courage. The friend of a friend of a friend could say anything and it wouldn't hurt. "You know Louise?"

She looks up, unsmiling, confused. "Louise – oh, right." She glances over to where our merry hostess is trying to clean up the mess as it's made, panic starting to eat into her eyes. "Not her, no. I'm not here for her."

"Oh?" I settle, leaning back against the kitchen island so that I'm almost facing her. "Someone else, then?"

"Yes." She digs in the pocket of her red coat, and I hear a skittery rustling like insects crawling over each other in the dark. She pulls out a folded piece of paper, thick and torn at the edges. "Janine."

Odd thing to do. "Yeah, I know her –"

"Russell," she continues, "Tracy, Benjamin." She folds the paper up again, sets it back in her pocket. "I'm a little early," she says with a shrug. "It happens. The department isn't exactly run by geniuses."

I take another sip from my coke. It's rum-sweet, and it's the only way this conversation will make sense. "Ben," I tell her. "No one calls me Benjamin."

The girl's face changes. Where before she had looked bored, a little out of place, now she looks completely other. It passes in a millisecond, just a flash where for a moment she wasn't sulky and young, but ageless, her skin like drying fish scales, hair made of knotted darkness. "Dammit," she says. "I thought you were – never mind. That shouldn't happen. Not today. You can't be on two lists, though it explains why you can see me."

"Can't I?" I finish my coke. The room is swimmy and strange, and

I have to focus, to keep her at the centre of my world. Of course I can see her, it's the only way the universe stays in place. "What's your name?"

"Jordan," she says. "Like the river."

"Yeah? Your parents all crazy religious?" Mine are, so I know how that story goes. I need another drink, but I don't want to leave Jordan, half-convinced that if I turn my back on her she'll slip away. I scan the counters – someone's left a half-finished beer and I take it, checking first that they haven't used it as an ashtray.

"I forget," Jordan says. She finally takes a drag of her cigarette, and when she does, she seems to become more real. More there. "Maybe."

Now there's an opening to a conversation if ever I saw one, but I'm not stupid enough to take it. You gotta be careful with those kind of statements. I make them myself. I open the door wide enough to see who will walk forward before I slam it in their face. "So what two lists am I on?"

"Dead and Deader," she says, and sticks out her tongue. "Forget it. You can only be on one."

"You're crazy," I tell her, as if she hasn't noticed. "It's a good crazy. Manic pixie dream girl goes Goth"

"Deader," she says. "I'm putting you on deader. That's for insulting me."

"I was trying to chat you up, not insult you." The beer tastes awful, like something died in it. I grimace and push myself away from her so I can go pour the rest down the drain. I need to sober up, anyway. Gotta get home. Russell's lifting me and if I get back to the house smelling like alcohol, and obviously drunk, I'll be asking for it. "Where do you think they keep the coffee?"

"There." Jordan points to a corner cupboard with the remains of her cigarette. It's almost out. "And the mugs are in that one." She points to another cupboard. "Milk is in the fridge." She flicks the stompie vaguely in the direction of the bin. I don't see it land.

"Milk I could have worked out for myself." But I'm grinning. I like her. I select two cups – one black and one white, both with cartoon red hearts on them. Tacky shit. "How do you take yours?"

"I don't –" She glances up at the clock that resembles a giant Marie biscuit stuck to the wall. "Oh, what the hells, it's not like I'm in a hurry.

Lots of milk, three sugars."

We drink our opposite-world coffees, looking at each other and saying nothing. She doesn't smile, and I like that. I like how she looks unfriendly and spiky and full of hate all while drinking something sweeter than melted ice cream and milkier than baby porridge. I like how the kitchen lights make her look like she's crowned in stars, and the shadows splay around her like vulture feathers. I like how she reminds me of falling.

"Don't get in the car," she says, and puts down her empty cup. "I'll give you time to say goodbye."

She comes back for me. After the crash.

"Deader, remember?" Jordan takes my hand and she's not cold, or warm, or anything. It's like holding smoke. "We always need replacements. Deaths get lost all the time. It's a long stretch between here and there, and some of us go missing in the dark."

"I – what?"

"You saw me." She's serious, brow pinched. "No one sees the Deaths, unless they've been put on the shortlist. Or, you know, just after." She looks away, and her hands are strong as claws, there's no escaping her. "It won't be so bad. It's not like dying."

"Really." It's all I can say. My throat is tight, it feels like it does after I've been choked. This is not how things were meant to go. I was going to leave home, put myself through university, get a decent job. "How's that?" When I move, my skin sounds like the sawing of cicadas, the shriek of a million locusts.

"Oh, dying always ends," she says. "It's Death that takes forever."

A psychopomp story, or, how a boy at a party avoids death and becomes a Death.

The Face of Jarry

The beach was empty. People don't like to walk their dogs so far down the strand, especially after that woman got murdered. A group of kids stabbed her to death for her mobile phone. Part of me really hoped it was an iPhone or something and she didn't die over a crappy Pep-store entry level Android. Because that would have sucked. I mean, it sucked anyway, but you know.

It was an early morning phone call with my mother that had driven me here. The same tail-devouring conversation: questions about the ex, how I could look prettier if I made a little more effort. A numb circle of repetition that had me running, as usual, trying to escape the purgatory of my mother's disappointment.

The sand was cold under my feet. I'd shucked my battered slops and tossed them in my sling bag, and all around me the beach was damp and strange. Mist rolled in off the grey waters and the waves gnashed white teeth that I could just glimpse now and again through the low bank of clouds. It was coming in thick and fast, and I had to watch my feet as I strode in order to not trip over the hillocks of storm-spat kelp that littered the coast. They stretched out in sepia glyphs, in a language I could almost understand. I closed my eyes and they stayed in my vision, bright and strobing, the aftershocks of dreams.

The feeling was sudden and intense: that if I took a moment, I could read this sea-writing and know the secrets that came from the deep. A cold sharpness, marrow-deep, and it passed so quickly that I had to laugh in case I thought I was going mad. I had to mock myself. Not that it made me feel any better, but there's something about getting in the first hit against yourself that's always felt satisfying to me. No one can tear me down more than I do myself. It's an idiot's armour against the world.

In trying to escape my mother's stupid call, I'd walked almost to the river mouth. A handful of cuttlefish bones were scattered near the shoreline and a dead gannet lay with its beak pointing to the sky like a bleached sentinel.

No roving gangs of murdering children, though. So that was a bonus.

The river water here was grit-filled, dirty with silt, but even so, I hopped off the edge of the crumbing sand bank and stood thigh deep in the cold rush of the estuary flow. I'd stepped into some other world. Not here, not there. Not anywhere.

I wished I could stay.

With a deep breath, I turned around to walk back home and the mist billowed like a new sail, revealing three shapes staggering a little way from me, leaning against the wind as they crossed the dunes. I yelped in fear, and one ash-grey figure turned his muted face to me, his horns iron dark, curling like a ram's. I'd seen these three figures before, still and naked and robbed of speech, sitting on a bench in the art gallery.

My heart stuttered. Some kind of Cape Town artistic statement, like the cowled death in a boat on Liesbeek River. A bunch of university brats dressed up as the Butcher Boys.

Fuck them. I had to get home and catch a train into town. I still had the afternoon shift to prep for. Even here in the long lonely places, I wasn't going to get to run away from myself.

It was in the news the next morning. How unknown thieves had broken into the gallery and somehow made off with the Butcher Boys. Everyone seemed bewildered by the why as much as the how. Students, I thought again, and spent the rest of the week running coffees and cakes for sweating tourists with wide American accents, dressed in safari gear in an air-conditioned shopping mall. I didn't have the time or energy to notice any more talk about the stolen sculpture.

I heard about Jarry on the train a few days later. The Southern line had broken down just outside Dieprivier, and I was packed in with a million other sweaty souls, wondering if this was hell or purgatory and deciding it was probably purgatory because hell would smell like brimstone not sun-warm piss and cheese Nik-Naks and dead things. The weather had turned strangely humid for summer, making everyone sticky-tired and mildew-scented. A constant shrieking hum razored the air like an army of invisible cicadas, fungus growing in odd places. Just the other day I had opened my tea tin to find a collection of silvery pearls – snail eggs – buried in among the composting oolong.

Now I was crushed on a graffitied seat on the train, hugging my laptop bag to my chest, my earphones buried in my ears like a protective ward against unwanted conversation and the interminable buzz, trying to avoid breathing too deeply, and half-listening to the jabber around me.

A million different languages spilling like warm wax, and the word that hooked me, that made me sit up a little straighter and almost forget the stench and the lateness and the sweat gathering like slug slime under my tee-shirt, the word that almost made me forget about my shitty life – the word was Jarry.

Two men were standing close to me and their voices were a little different from everyone else's. Maybe that's what caught my attention. They spoke English as if it were a foreign language, with a lilt and cadence I'd never heard before. I tried to place them. Tourists, certainly. From where?

"The old way into Jarry is closed now," said the one with his back to me. "The dream is ended."

His companion, who had eyes like bright dark fish, looked as if he was having stomach troubles. He winced. "There will be other ways in. I'm sure of it."

"And if there were – do we want to go back? How long before we forget who we are, become part of the Long Road and see nothing more of this world? Perhaps it's better to stay here with the apes."

Were they rehearsing some kind of play? That had to be it. Actors using the wasted time on a stuck train to learn their lines.

The dream is ended. I wondered what the play was about.

Then a screech, a lurch, and the chuff-chuff-chuff of the groaning train as we set on our way once more. I glanced down at my watch. Forty-five minutes late. When I looked up, the men were moving, pushing their way through the crowd toward the end of the carriage. No more talk of Jarry and the Long Road. I settled back and closed my eyes. Maybe I'd catch some sleep before Valsbaai.

Jarry crawled into my head after that. I looked for it in dreams, in books abandoned yellowly in the leaf-clogged gutters, in the calligraphy of dead jellyfish, in the seal corpses that washed up stinking from the storms. But Jarry, whatever it was, remained as incomprehensible as the strange weather. My mother called two days after my birthday to ask if I could look something up on 'the Google' for her. Instead I searched for Jarry, for a play about dreams, but there was nothing.

I forgot.

It was almost a month later when I saw the girl with the sign. Normally, I ignore people-with-signs. It's not that I'm a complete shit, it's just that I have only so many R5 coins to give out and after a while the eye contact makes me feel guilty. And sure, I am guilty. Too rich in a world where most people are pretty much starving.

The girl was standing in the middle of the road, on the yellow-painted island, the sign around her neck on a piece of twine. She was staring blindly ahead and the wind from the passing cars whipped her hair around her head in a fury.

She wasn't asking for money or hand-outs or anything. The sign just said:

JARRY!!!
FIND A NEW ROAD BEFORE THE JESUS COMES
JARRY!!!

Normally, I'd hurry past people like her, with her grime and her sour smell and her madness like a blanket all tucked up around her, but instead I waited for the lights to turn red, then darted through the stalled traffic. She didn't flinch as I came close, didn't flinch or wheedle or beg. She ignored me.

"Hi," I said. "Um, so, Jarry?"

The lights changed, cars revved and roared, rubbish smacked around our heels. Someone yelled something out of his car window as he passed us, but the wind dragged it away.

"On your sign?" I tapped the word. The first Jarry with its eleventy-billion exclamation marks, each drawn with a meticulous neatness in purple kokie pen. "What is it? Like, a place or something?"

I was starting to feel more than a little stupid. Her pale eyes were turned to the horizon and she didn't blink. What the hell had possessed me to come and make idle chit-chat to some weirdo with a sign anyway? A Jesus-freak with a sign, I should clarify. At least she wasn't trying to convert me or get me to repent or cower from some non-existent end-times.

"Yeah," I said. "Never mind." And just because I guess I wanted to throw her a little, to get some kind of reaction I said: "The dream has ended, anyhow."

She moved so fast I didn't even have time to stumble backwards or dodge. Her hand shot out and caught my wrist, fingers cold and tight like the rusted jaws of a pair of old pliers. "What do you know about Dreaming?" Her breath was cold. We were standing on a traffic island under a baking Cape Town summer sun and her breath was ice.

"Nothing." I shook my hand free. "Nothing, forget it, lady."

She shoved me hard in the chest, almost sending me backward into the traffic. "Stay away from Jarry, ape," she said. "Stay in your own stinking shit and misery."

I didn't have time for this. All I'd wanted was a litre of milk and a pack of Camels and to get back to my apartment where it was marginally cooler and I had a lifetime supply of illegally downloaded TV-series that would probably only make it to South Africa in 3011. Jarry, cold breath and the Jesus. Apes. Just... nonsense words. Meaning nothing. I shook it away and ran.

By the time I got home, I'd played that damn encounter in my head a million times. It wasn't as if I could talk to anyone about it. Savvie was at work and she'd probably call me an idiot for 'making first contact' anyway.

I could Tweet about how some crazy on the street just about gave me a one way trip to the Saviour himself, or I could see if any of my friends were online and maybe I could mention something, because I couldn't get her words scraped out from my skull.

Not nonsense. True words.

I knew nothing about dreaming. I never remembered mine. So instead of talking to anyone, I smoked cigarettes because a girl has to have vices and I watched a show I'd already seen because the actors were adorable and the hoyay was strong, and I Instagrammed Savvie's cat because it was Saturday.

My hands shook. I smoked more cigarettes and pretended everything was okay.

What else was I supposed to do?

I met The Jesus in a bar, while I was busy turning wine into water. Snap. I was there alone because Sav had bailed on me, claiming that working in a bar had put her off them for life. Odd thing. So I'd left her with the cat and headed down the road to the only mildly grotty Hole, got drunk enough to not care that I was a frumpy mother's failure, and found myself a skinny pretty Jesus.

He was haloed under a lamp that curved down like a curious tulip, drinking something clear and sparkly from a glass frosted with tiny droplets. It's not as if I was at the Hole trying to get laid, of course. More like, I was open to the opportunity if it arose. Ha ha, so many terrible puns. But that's the reason I noticed him. I'm a sucker for a pretty face. Envy, maybe.

And he was all Pretty Face. One of those boys that looks like he's just waiting for the 80s to resurface so that he can dig out his mother's clothing. A long face and hair that stood out in every direction, a perfect collusion of natural curl and expensive product.

He was sketching. And it should have felt so put-on, so damnably coy and pretentious. So look-at-me. Somehow it didn't. I took a seat close to him and ordered another glass of the house red (boxed; I'm no fool, but then again I don't come to the Hole to satisfy my exquisitely refined palate) and watched as his pencil danced across the paper, leaving a shadowy image behind.

"Did you draw that from your head?" Stupid question. It must have been. It's not as if there was a three-headed dog sprawled out on the bar-counter.

Pretty Face looked up and he had a startled look, the sort I imagined a deer would have, if I'd ever seen a deer. I saw a porcupine once. It's not quite the same thing, saying someone had a startled look like a porcupine. That's a totally different kind of startled.

One where you get a face full of black and white spines.

"I –" He just sort of sat there. Looking for an escape route, possibly. There would have been an awkward silence. Instead there was just an awkward mumbly indie guitar with whispery vocals.

So, All Pretty Face and No Pretty Brains. I was already spilling over with disappointment. At least the wine was good. What am I saying – the wine was terrible.

"No," he said.

Terrific. Forward motion on the conversation train. I put down my glass. "Uh-huh."

"I saw one once."

I wanted to laugh at him, to mock him before he could mock me, but he had this serious cast to his face, a sweet sort of innocence that made me bite back on whatever scathing retort I was fermenting. "In your dreams?" I said instead.

He laughed. It was a nice sound, all smoky and warm, like the last hour of a good party. "In the Dreaming."

"In Jarry," I snapped back, as if the word had been sitting curled up on the back of my tongue, just waiting for the moment I would let it free.

"Yes," he said.

After a few seconds he closed his sketchbook, downed the last of his drink and took my hand. I let him, not because I'm an idiot, but because Jarry had already eaten into my dreams and I desperately wanted to go there.

We walked out into a night that had turned shivery; a cold front blowing in from the ocean. I rubbed my hands along my arms and watched him, watched his breath smoking. He was real. I didn't even know his name. I was drunk. Maybe.

Probably. You should phone Sav, I told myself.

"So," I said. "You know how to get to Jarry."

He was fiddling with his jacket zip. It had got caught in the strap of his little flat portfolio bag. "I did once," he muttered.

"But the old ways are closed."

"Yes." He looked up at me, frowning. He was even prettier when he frowned. It gave him the air of a confused lizard. "How do you know?"

I shrugged.

"Because you don't smell like someone who has been to Jarry."

"I do this thing. It's called bathing."

"No –" He brought one hand to his face, and covered his right eye. The other one stared at me unblinking. A little creepy, I'll admit. But we were still standing outside the Hole. There were people around. "You look wrong."

"Nice. I already get that shit from my mother. I don't need it from you." I turned to stagger back and he caught my arm, gently pulling me to him.

"Not – not like that." He smiled, shy as a schoolboy on a first date.

"Your face is perfect."

Perfect. I'm an idiot, but it was still nice to hear a little flattery for a change.

"I meant," he said, "that you don't look like someone who has seen Jarry." His hand was melting-warm on my cold arm and, just for once, I wanted to hold on to the idea that something about me was worthwhile, even if I knew he was lying. And I wanted to know more. So sue me. "I haven't." I sighed. "Obviously."

"Ah." He lowered his hand, held it out to me. "I'm Sullivan. And I can get you there."

Pretty Face, Pretty Hands. Long fingers. Elegant. Fingers that could draw the strange, the magical. Of course I shook his hand. "Euphemia," I said. "Shut up, my parents were weird, you get used to it. Call me Mia if the whole thing is too much."

"Euphemia."

"Exactly."

"It sounds like a drug."

I laughed. "Oh, hang on, is that what this is? Is Jarry a trip?"

"Yes," said Sullivan. "The best." Then he shook his head. "It's not – it's better than drugs. It's marvellous."

I'm not even going to pretend I wasn't having massive second-thoughts by this point.

"There are still ways into Jarry, there always are, but the main portico collapsed, so everyone ape-side is trying to find a new way back and it's all a bit chaotic right now..." He waved his Pretty Hands around.

"Ape-side?"

"Where the humans live."

"Ah." I edged sideways. It was too cold out here anyway. Chatting with Pretty Face Sullivan had been entertaining, but we were now steering the Good Ship Conversation far past the Harbour of Mildly Amusing into the uncharted Seas of Uncomfortably Weird. "Perfect."

"You can't help being human," and he said it so sincerely. Perhaps it was his voice. I was being hypnotised. That's it. Totally hypnotised. "It's not your fault."

"Ah." My conversational train had derailed. I didn't exactly have a lot of responses ready for this sort of thing. "What are you then?"

"A go-between." When he smiled, I swear it all made sense. "Now, come on. There's supposed to be a slipway to Jarry here, but it's temperamental at best. Takes a bit of thumping before it works."

"And you know this how?" I followed him, every molecule of my brain screaming, but damn me, I followed him anyway. "I thought you'd only used the Old Way."

"An angel told me."

"Right. Angel." I nodded.

"Yes, exactly. Zaile. He was drunk at the time and I had to trade him a starling-bowl for the information, but Zaile's Mundus-born." He was smiling again. "It will be there, and we will get it to work."

"Okay." I was fumbling with my phone, sending a message to Sav. *Near Hole. Chatting up weirdo. Pretty weirdo. Possible serial killer. Pretty serial killer. Not home in twenty send heavily-armed men.* "So how far is this doorway-thing?"

He stopped. We were literally half a block from the Hole. I could still see people lounging on the pavement, leaning against the walls, talking shit and smoking and drinking their craft beers. Safe. "Right here."

I tilted my head. Someone had stuck a poster to the wall. It was for a circus. Last year. Most of the poster was gone. Some scrawled graffiti, a damp patch that smelled like urine and a few weeds growing through the cracks. "It's... wonderful," I said. "I'm truly lost for words."

Sullivan slammed his open palm into the center of the crumbling brick wall, and I jumped. Beneath his hand, the wall shivered. Sullivan grinned.

And I saw Jarry.

It was night over the city and the stars hung in garlands across the sky, stars of silver and blue and red and green, like distant fireworks. The buildings were tall and narrow teeth, blackened in the indigo maw of the sky. It wasn't the sight of Jarry that made me draw a deep breath, like an infant's first, but the smell.

Incense and jungle green and parrot feather sweetness and a cinnamony musk, the air of a different world. Behind me, the Hole and the stink of beer and cigs, salt and stale fish faded, the empty ocean night falling away. I didn't even have to wait for Sullivan to speak, I stepped forward before anyone or anything could stop me.

The air was thicker here and my lungs had to work harder to draw forth oxygen. I took gulping breaths, filling my chest with a sweet taste that reminded me of pears soaked in whisky.

"Jarry," said Sullivan, and his voice was loaded with emotion. I tried to place it. Relief? Perhaps. It was flooded with something close to tears, as if it had been years since he had seen the city and was finally coming home.

"Oh my god," I said. "It's real. It's really real."

Sullivan didn't acknowledge me, probably because yes, it was really real and I was stating the fucking obvious. In my hand, my phone had gone dead – not just out of signal range or emergency call only, but utterly black. I thumbed the power button a few times, but nothing happened. With a short sigh of irritation I slipped the phone back into my pocket. Of course I wanted to Instagram this shit; it was the most exciting thing to happen to me since forever.

The skyline grew clearer as my eyes adjusted to the new world and the strange starlight. One of the buildings towered over the other, a huge window that resembled a rose flowering on one side. We might not have churches quite like that in South Africa, but I'd have to be completely illiterate to not know a cathedral when I see one. It was massive though, far larger than anything I'd ever imagined.

"So the church even made it to other worlds?" I said, one finger pointed to the monstrosity. As if Sullivan wouldn't know what I was talking about.

He laughed. "The Cathedral still hangs onto its dreams of a new Jesus, but they're waiting for nothing."

"You know that personally, do you? The Almighty drop you a line?"

Sullivan took my arm. "Even if there is one, he won't bother coming here. This is just a way-stop, a place where the lost souls drift. Purgatory, if you will."

"So why the hell did you want to get back?"

"There's something I need." He fumbled in his coat. "Listen, it's not exactly safe for you here. Stay too long and you'll forget you were ever anywhere else, and then you'll become part of the Long Road and never get back home."

"Whoa – wait. What?"

He took a small blue egg out of his pocket and cradled it in his palm. "I can anchor you to Earth, but you'll need to swallow this."

"You're kidding."

"Hardly." He pressed the egg into my hand.

It wasn't actually an egg, just a tiny pale stone, no bigger than the nail of my pinkie. I closed my fist around it. Cold. And hard. Small enough to swallow whole. "And you want me to actually put this in my mouth –?" I began.

"The sooner the better." His eyes were fierce and dark here under the rainbow stars. "You really don't have much time." His look softened. "Sorry, Mia. I'm worried. If you're trapped here, it would be on me, all that guilt. I simply took you, didn't warn you or anything. Please, for your own safety."

The egg tasted of nothing. Just a moment's flinty coolness, and then I swallowed it down like I was taking a handful of painkillers the morning after the night before, dry and desperate.

I imagined that it sat heavy in my stomach, connecting me back to earth, but in reality I could feel nothing at all. "You're sure it will work?"

"Yes," he said and his smile grew warmer, grateful almost. "Beyond certain." He grabbed my arm. "And now, we'd best move, if I'm to make my appointment."

I shook off his grip, but followed him anyway. Sullivan was walking briskly down a narrow road edged on either side by delicate spindly buildings draped in what looked like fairy lights. As I passed, I saw that they were all mismatched – some antique glass bulbs that looked older than dust, and some new and cheap, the kind you get at China Town for a couple of twenties.

"Detritus," said Sullivan. "Stolen dreams."

"What's that supposed to mean?"

"Some of the more unusual residents can slip off the Long Road, into what they call Dreaming. Back into your world. And it is your world, to an extent." He glanced back at me. "It was your world."

"They... go back in time?"

"About fifteen minutes or so behind, yes. They take what they can, and bring it back here to trade. There are also a few doorways that do the same thing, but they're expensive to use."

"Oh." I didn't really have anything intelligent to say, I realised, but just about none of this made any sense. It had all the logic of a dream. I wasn't convinced that I was not actually dreaming. The whole thing had taken on a menacing eeriness: things brought back from the past, dream-nonsense and doorways to other worlds.

We walked the city of Jarry, heads bowed as though we didn't want anyone to notice us. I saw things, of course. I couldn't help staring. Women dressed in bearskins, their great ursine heads like bizarre frightening helmets, men in sackcloth and ashes, wearing gilded crosses almost as big as my hand, people with thin faces, their eyes like shifting mist. Three ashy figures wearing curling horns, naked, their mouths sealed. Butchers. They nodded at me as I passed, their black eyes full of secrets they couldn't tell me.

I didn't think I liked Jarry very much. My hand pressed against my stomach, just under my ribs. Staying here was becoming less and less appealing. Sullivan's egg had better work.

Finally, Sullivan led me to a small arched door sunk halfway into the ground, down a little half-flight of stairs marked in a checkerboard pattern. There was a painted wooden sign just above the door, swinging idly in the faintly perfumed breeze.

Die Eend en Esel.

"Tell me purgatory is not full of repressed Afrikaans Calvinists," I said. "The Duck and Donkey? Really?"

"It's as good a name as any and, besides, you can be sure that no one here even remembers what it means. It's gibberish from the past. Probably stolen," Sullivan added. He stepped down and pushed the door open. Chatter and smoke and the rapid scrape and whine of a fiddle spilled out into the night. "Come along," he said. "We're letting the stink out."

Inside Die Eend en Esel the crowd were mussels in a tide pool, shoulder to shoulder, pressed thick and black and salty, their voices and laughs braying and rolling. People were dressed in mismatched fashions, as if they'd raided a garage sale black bag of unwanted clothes and tried them on with no regard for style or colour or, indeed, anything. One tall woman was wearing a curtain tie-back as a necklace, the tassel hanging between her breasts like a tired dancer.

Sullivan elbowed his way toward the back of the pub, and I trailed in his wake, muttering excuse-mes to no one who was listening.

Finally, we came to another door, this one closed. A few raps and a hurried exchange, and we were in, the door shut behind us and the noise muffled.

"No," said a small man, sitting on a stool in front of a large wardrobe. "It doesn't matter what you pay me, it's not going to work. Passage to Mundus is beyond your reach, not with that face." He took off the long top hat he was wearing and squinted. "What's this you brought?"

"Tor."

"Sullivan." The man rolled his hat in his hands, his eyes glinting as he looked at me. "Answer the question."

"A way in."

He shook his head. "Oh no. The gates won't open for you and you know it. Mundus is closed to your signature."

Sullivan shrugged. "I'm aware of that. I'm also an avid reader, and a great follower of various Mundus-collectors and what they keep in stock." He pulled a second little blue egg stone out of his jacket pocket, and held it out between finger and thumb.

My stomach began to feel heavier, as if that stone was growing in my body, weighing me down like a cat in a sack ready to be drowned. Sweat filmed my forehead and neck, despite the fact I was shivering. I wanted to run, but where to? It occurred to me that, even with this egg, I had no idea how to return to Earth. My tongue was dry and heavy; my mouth filled with old meat.

Tor looked from Sullivan to me, his face twisted in thought, then he turned away from us and unlatched the closet. The doors fell open, revealing a gauzy mist. On the interior walls were strange maps, marked here and there with rusted pins. "Well, you won't need these, you're going off-map," he said as he fiddled with the tacks, moving them about until they formed a small pattern on the very edge of the map, in a blank and empty nowhere. "This won't be cheap," he added over his shoulder.

"I expected as much." Sullivan leaned against one smoky wall and chewed at his thumbnail. "You want something from Mundus, right?"

"Yes, and nothing too common, you hear? I'm taking a risk with you, cuckoo-stone or no."

"Cuckoo stone?" I'd found my voice.

"This." Sullivan twisted his hand, palming the little egg and bringing it up toward my face. It was identical to mine in every way, down to the faint speckled pattern. "See," he said, and he took my hand in his free one, his palm hot and dry and comforting against my skin. He clasped his fingers in mine, as if we were lovers. "I'm not exactly allowed into Mundus. Or, at least, my body isn't." He clapped his hand over his mouth, and his throat worked as he swallowed his own cuckoo stone dry.

The feeling started in my stomach. My actual stomach, not my guts. A sudden hot pain like an ulcer. I doubled over, trying to pull myself free of Sullivan's grip but he only held tighter. I was sure his fingers were going to leave bruises between my knuckles. I wrenched harder but his hand was like iron.

No, like my own skin. It felt as if I were trying to tear off a piece of my own flesh. I twisted, looked up at him.

His face shifted.

Every bone in my body cracked, snapped, lengthened and thickened. I felt myself growing heavier and taller and different.

And Sullivan grew smaller, his pretty-Jesus mask disappearing into a face I have grown up with, grown bored with, learned to almost-tolerate.

"What the shit?" I said slowly, and my voice was deeper, rough like smoke and barbed like wire. Sullivan's voice.

"Cuckoo stone," said Tor, helpfully. "He's kicking you out of your flesh-nest." He was still standing at the open closet. Behind him the gauzy portal-thing had started to thin, and I could just make out a huge onion-bulbed dome of a building. "Right by The Circus," he added, to Sullivan. To Sullivan, who looked exactly like me. A plainjane, a nothing, a forgettable face, one that would attract the attention of no one. "Couldn't have asked for a better place. Right in the thick of it." Tor grinned. His teeth were small and even and yellowed. "I better get something good out of this, Sully, old lad."

"Call me Mia," the girl said. My voice sounded higher and sweeter than I'd thought it actually did. Like hearing myself recorded. Mia let go of my hand and I fell backwards, all the strength gone from me. I was left crumpled on the floor, barely able to move.

That's not me. It didn't matter what I thought – it looked like me, down to the swollen scratch on my neck where I'd been bitten by a mosquito last night. It was me. Without any actual me-ness inside.

The Mia-Sullivan-thing dusted its hands down its new body and frowned momentarily before its face brightened. "Excellent." Flushed with an eager light, it stepped toward the portal and brushed fingers down the thinning veil. The grey mist parted, rolling back to reveal the onion-dome building clearly. From what I could tell, the portal had opened in a doorway in a narrow street. It was shaded, and humid air seemed to seep into Tor's little room.

"Mundus," Mia-Sullivan said. "Oh, you beauty." And stepped through.

Now I walk the Long Road in a skin that is prettier than any I have ever owned. Sullivan's face and voice plastered over me. I walk alone. Except for the mute Butcher Boys, who recognize something in me, some sea-side speck of a city they half-remember. They cannot talk to me, and no one else will. With my pretty-Jesus face, with my long artist's hands, I am not welcome in Jarry. I try to follow the caravans of the Dreamers, hoping that one of them will dream me a way back home, but the years crawl past and I have forgotten the shapes of the kelp language and the spell I want to draw me once more to my ocean.

I walk the purgatory ring-road between the sound of the sea and the promise of a stranger heaven, my phone held out before me, waiting for some signal to shine in its black face. But I already know the dream is ended.

"The Face of Jarry" originally appeared in a Lovecraft anthology, which just goes to show that you don't have to do Cthulhu-esque pastiche for people to recognise your influences. It's set initially in Muizenberg, where I lived, and those beaches are mine. I've walked them. I have not been to Jarry, however.

The Worme Bridge

When I was old enough to walk by myself to the shops to buy my mother her cigarettes, she decided I was too old to believe in rubbish like Santa Claus and the tooth mouse and fairies that live at the bottom of the garden. Instead, I would learn the real stuff, such as what really happened to Pa and my older brother Matty, and what was going to happen to her.

Why ever since Pa had died she'd made me take him as medicine, ground up into my food to ward off the sickness.

Ma couldn't walk properly because her feet pained her now that they'd gone all boneless and scaly with sickness, and no one would serve Matthias because of the stink, even if he could have walked to the shops himself. Which he couldn't. Matty was born like that, though, Ma told me, with his legs all melted together like two candles lit too close to each other and forgotten.

The trips weren't so bad. I liked the walk past all the square little houses with their concrete ox-wagon wheel walls, with their laundry and their chimney smoke, flicking the lighter in my pocket and thinking about things to burn. I liked to pretend no one saw me, walking up to the corner shop where the Indian men would sell me cigarettes even if I was only ten, because they knew my ma and I guess they felt sorry for her. The walk there and back took twice as long as it should have because I had to go to the second-closest shop. The closest one meant going riverwise and crossing the foot bridge built in 1809 and named after some dead man, I guess the one who built it in 1809. Or maybe he just had other people build it in 1809. He was very proud of it because he put a big stone right by the front that said Built in 1809 so we would never forget. The man was called Matthias too, but they called the bridge Worme instead.

By the time I got back to Ma, I'd always be wishing she didn't have these rules about the bridge and the river. Some days it could get so hot the tar would melt under your feet and give you new soles for free, and sometimes it was so cold you wouldn't even be sure you had feet and would have to check at the door before going into the house. Are these feet inside my shoes? Or have I got the sickness too?

Let me tell you for nothing it was a great relief to find all my toes in the right order and with the right amount of skin and bone. You miss them fierce when you don't have them.

I would open Ma's cigarette box for her while she shivered, wrapped in dog blankets she bought cheap at the Pick n Pay. The skin on her hands hurt too much to do it herself. I loved that crinkle of the see-through plastic, thin as sleep, the slow tear. I loved peeling back the silvery paper and finding the twenty sticks, all neat as soldiers. The smell of new tobacco, before the fire ate it. I would breathe deeply, then pick the bottom middle one to draw out. The virgin straw.

If it had been my box of smokes, I would have taken that one and turned it over and placed it back in, filter face out. I am old enough to know about virgins, but too old for fairies.

Ma was always like that – telling me what it was time for me to believe in. I knew about virgins because one time she decided I needed god, or we all did, so she took me and Matty to the church – rolling him all the way there on a low wooden trolley with wheels from a pram. We had to sit on cold hard pews and listen to the man at the top tell us stuff from the Bible. This was when Matty was alive, of course. We didn't take his stinking twisted body to church after, even though they seem to love believing in dead guys.

It was boring in the church and because Matty couldn't sit properly, he was rolling around on the pew and flopping about and just being a general nuisance, so people kept looking at us and whispering and shaking their heads. It was also because Ma was single. I had a dad but he died before Matty was born so it was hard to explain to people how that worked. They thought Ma was a whore. Another word I was old enough to know.

Except for all the idiots, there was one nice thing, and that was the singing. During the boring bits the man at the top would say everybody rise and turn in your hymn-books to page and every person who still had their body would shuffle up with whispers and cracks and rustle through their pages until they found the right one. Not Matty, he just rolled about, gasping because he already couldn't breathe properly then. But I would stand up, and Ma next to me, and we would share this hymn-book which was a thick book with pages made of fairy wings. We joined together in praise of our good risen lord, who I guess was Jesus or his dad, since they were actually the same person. And this Jesus guy was dead and then alive again, and all the church people were okay with that and made songs about it. So you can see why I didn't understand why they could deal with Jesus being dead, but they couldn't deal with Pa or Matty.

The music was slow and sad and filled with water, and it was like drowning, but nicer. There was an old lady who would play this organ, which was a big thing like a piano but with a different sound, a sound of waves. It made music that crashed down right over your head. Then all the cold deep men's voices rose up with currents and little waves and eddies of higher sounds, like water that is warm in the sun.

And I would sing too, catching the tune and letting it pull me on, the notes flickers of fish, shoals of bright sounds that raced through the river of the organ swell. And that's how I know about virgins because they kept going on about Jesus' ma being a virgin and my ma had to explain it there in the church because I kept asking.

And then one day Ma decided we didn't need god after all and we stayed home on Sundays again. She had to drown Matty and there's no way to explain that kind of thing to church people.

"Sanette? Is that you?" Ma called from inside the house even though no one else ever comes to us. I sighed and kicked off my shoes so I could unroll my socks and check my toes. It was winter – the third after Ma took Matty to the river and the second after her own feet gave in. All my toes were present, which is what you say at school when the teacher calls your surname in home class.

I always get called last: "Worme."

And my answer is to say: "Present, mejevrou." As if I am giving her a gift, which I am not, unless it is the gift of my presence, which is a pun, Matty says. Also I must call her mejevrou even though it is an English school because she says *mis* is what cows make.

I wriggled all my toes, one by one. "Ja, Ma," I said. Then I frowned, because the one pinky toe was stiff and a little blue, but I couldn't tell if that was because of winter, or because I was going down the road of illness. Ma had always said that I would be fine because my legs were straight and strong, and it was only the boys who have to be drowned and brought back. But that was before her feet went, so now I am extra scared all the time.

Quickly, I covered up my toes, rubbed them hard to make them warm, and shoved them back in my school shoes, which were black and pretty with a strap and a floral cut-out and were more expensive than plain Mary Janes. I had feet, so all the shoe money went on me.

"I got your cigarettes, Ma." I grabbed the plastic bag back up. Cigs for Ma, a Kit Kat for me and tin of sardines for Matty. I hopped over the little ridge of wood on the front door step, and went inside.

The smell was very bad in my house. Partly that was because of Matty, but also Ma who sat with her feet in a black plastic tub of hot water and her dog blankets wrapped around her, hoping to stay human, and partly it was because she kept Pa's bones. Though they were dried out now, they still had a funny stink to them, like the skin of a snake or a lizard. They were in a box covered with sea shells and lined inside with red felt. A very expensive box – almost a hundred rand – but not very big, because there weren't so many bones left. Ma kept grinding them up and feeding them to me.

"Here," I said, unwrapping the box of cigarettes as slowly as I could. I folded the silver paper neatly and tucked it in my blazer pocket, took out the first virgin straw and lit it with my yellow lighter that I keep only for Ma's cigarettes, and not for anything else, like setting fire to the school dustbins. The smoke tasted like the death of fairies and Santa Claus. The smoke tasted like learning the truth and it always made me choke. I handed her the lit cig and crouched down to look at her feet.

They were going wrong. I didn't need to be a doctor to see they were turning long and thin and see-through like Matty's. The skin at her ankles was rubbery, melting together. There were raw bits shining pale red where she'd pulled the skin apart. It didn't matter. In a few months Ma would be as bad as Matty. She was already starting to smell rotten. Worse than cigarettes and not-washing. "You okay, Ma?"

She nodded, and blew out smoke so I couldn't see the expression in her eyes. She only started smoking when her feet started changing, and I think it was because she believed that the stink of the cigarettes covered up the other smell. Which was definitely getting worse. Maybe she and Matty couldn't tell because they were wrapped in it all day like a duvet, but I still went outside and knew that healthy people with two good strong legs did not smell like cod liver oil rotting inside a bottle left on a windowsill in the sun.

"Ma, where's Pa's old trolley?" I said, because at thirteen I was learning to be practical. We used the trolley to take Matty to school, and to church, and then, right at the end of his first life, to take him down to our family bridge built in 1809, which is probably when the first Worme had to drown someone in their family.

Ma coughed, choking on her stinking cigarette. "Don't need the trolley yet," she said and waved at her feet. "I'm fine now, the water's helping."

The water would only help with the pain for so long, we both knew. Towards the end, we kept Matty in the bath, trying to slow everything down with clean water, scraping off his scales and trying to cut his fingers apart. He used to cry when Ma took the little vegetable peeling knife and slit through the skin growing thin between his fingers, gluing them together. He never cried loud, but he turned his face to the wall and his shoulders would shake. Ma dropped the bits of skin in a plastic bowl that I held out for her, and then I buried them in the garden.

But even with all that cutting and burying, we couldn't stop his insides from changing, or help his lungs work. We had to drown him. It was the quickest way to set him free, in the end.

We'd gone at night, Matty crouched and covered with a sheet on his trolley, and rattle-bounced down the gritty tar road that was always full of potholes because of the summer rain, all the way to the river and the Worme Bridge.

Ma had drowned him. I had just sat on the edge of the river with my knees right up against my chest and cried, because ten is too young to know that sometimes your parents have to do what's best for you even if it hurts you. Even if it hurts them.

Afterwards we had dragged Matty back home, wrapped in his sheet again, and three days later he'd said he felt much better and he was sorry that Ma was so sad.

I watched Ma smoking her cigarettes and smelling like rancid fish, before I left her and went to the bathroom. The door was closed, so I knocked, and after a while Matty said to come in.

"How was school?" he asked. He could still talk, though it could be hard to make out the words unless you knew what he was saying. Also, he was really smelly. Not in a rotting way, like Ma, but like a harbour full of seals and seaweed.

"Okay," I told him. "You lucky you missed all this, I think this is the hundredth time we are learning about the Great Trek." Which is basically the story of how a bunch of Dutch people in the Cape got mad at the English and missioned off up the country, and mostly they had a horrible time of it but they said God was on their side so he helped them kill a lot of black people, which seems a bit unfair to the black people, really. This god guy, I don't know.

"I brought you something," I told him, and peeled open the tin of sardines.

Matty took them with a wide grin, which was horrible because all his teeth had fallen out and his mouth was full of needle white splinters. I was used to them, but I could imagine if anyone else had seen him they'd be grossed out. And scream, and probably try to bash his head in with a spade.

I waited till he finished his meal, dripping the last of the fishy oil down his throat, and handed me the empty tin before I told him about Ma.

He frowned. "I was wondering why she never came to visit me any more," he said, and I could hear how sad that made him. "Thought maybe she was sick of seeing me." He waved at his legs, which were under water, fused all together and silvery green and scarred with white ridges. In the beginning, Ma had tried to scrape the scales off with the back of a knife, but she gave up after he died and now they'd grown in funny. Some scales were beautiful silver and the size of my thumb nail, others were twisted and small and a dull grey. In places the scales never grew out at all, and the skin was white and puffy-raw. I knew they hurt him, those raw scars. We would never do that to Ma, but we couldn't stop her doing it to herself.

"She's definitely going funny," I said. I curled my toes in my shoes, and felt the one twinge and ache. Not me. I wasn't going. My legs were fine. I wasn't going to die. But Ma was. "I'll dig the trolley out of the garage tonight. We'll need it soon."

Matty didn't say anything after that, just swirled his webbed fingers through the little bit of water he could move in, and sighed deeply. Every now and again he would shift his body so that he could put his head under water for a moment to wet his gills. He could breathe out of water for a little while if he had to but preferred it the other way: gillwise.

I pulled the plug to drain some of the water, and ran in fresh cold water from the taps. Matty didn't feel the cold like I did. He said it was better, the cold. Being warm made breathing hard, even though he tried holding on to it, because it made him feel human still.

"If I have to drown Ma," I whispered to him, "you're going to have to move out to the river." There was only one bath in the Worme house. The Wormes who had died couldn't survive out of water. Just look at Pa. Or what was left of him.

"It won't be so bad," Matty said, which was a lie. Matty would be in the river, and Ma would live in the bath. And I – I would have to keep grinding up what was left of Pa and sprinkling him into my sandwiches to keep me from turning. I would have to buy Ma sardines with the little bit of money she kept under her mattress, and change her bath water, and watch her be alone and dead.

"If it happened to Ma," I said, "Chances are it will happen to me."

Even Matty couldn't lie that much, not right to my face. "Perhaps," he said. "But Ma is old, it only took her now. You've got years to live."

Years. A whole lifetime of living in the Worme house, with only my dead ma in the bath tub for company, and being able to spend time with my big brother only when there was no moon and I could pray to the dead Jesus who rose again that no one would see me sneak down to the river.

I took Matty down to the river first. Three months had gone past since we'd talked about killing Ma, and winter was softening a little at the edges. Ma could hardly breathe most of the time, and she'd stopped sending me out to buy her cigs. She'd turned down the last pack I bought, and I kept it now, sealed and new. As a reminder.

"It's time," I told him. "There's no moon tonight, and it'll be dark enough."

I could wheel Matty down on the trolley, wrapped in his sheet. He could breathe long enough for me to get him to the river, we knew that much. If people heard the midnight rattle of the pram wheels, they would just think it was some homeless guy, looking for junk, rooting through the rubbish bins. No one would come to see what I was doing.

We waited for the dark to fall and for the stars to light up. When there is no moon the stars shine much brighter, as though they're trying to make up for all the time the moon takes from them. When the cat's away the mice will play, I thought, and pictured the stars as little bright mice leaping here and there, looking for crumbs in the night. It was better than thinking about what we were going to do.

It was better than thinking about the toenail I found in my sock, and how my pinkie toe had started growing long and thin, and how I could see the bone through the skin, how it bent easily as the quill of a small feather. How spongey the skin on my legs felt.

I carried Matty, half-dragging him out to the trolley, and when he was firmly wrapped in place, I grabbed the thick plastic twine of the pull, feeling it bite into the softening skin of my palm, and tugged him down the road to the Worme Bridge. Matty went easily into the water, and stretched out, flicking the long bones of his feet. Of his tail. He belonged here. It would take a blind idiot to think he didn't. And Ma did too.

"I'll be back," I told him. He nodded. He'd promised to do the drowning. It would be easier for him, already there in the river. No sense getting me all wet and I'd already had to do all the heavy work of hauling both of them down to the water.

Ma didn't argue with me. Her legs were mostly grown together by now, and her feet were gone. Just a big split tail like a fish's stuck on all wrong. She'd given up on scraping away at her growing scales sooner than she'd given up on Matty's, so she was already silvering. Her legs were bare and sexless, but she wore a big loose tee shirt.

"I'm not about to go around naked like a whore," she told me. "I'll go to my death with dignity."

She was much heavier than Matty, though at least she was able to help me more. After a bunch of heaving and swearing we got her on to the trolley, and I started the final trek down, the trolley practically racing me so that I had to run to keep up with it and Ma, so that they didn't career off into the pavement and send Ma rolling downhill like a giant dead tuna.

I pulled the trolley to a stop near the bank, tearing open the puffy skin on my palms, and hobbled over to Ma to help her down to the water's edge. My new toe was paining me, crushed up in my shoe. Luckily we'd talked it all through before, the three of us, and Ma went to the water like a woman going to John the Baptist, who was a friend of Jesus and also had to drown him first.

It didn't take long, though she thrashed a fair bit while Matty held her under.

During their struggle, I kicked off my shoes and sat on the bridge, my bottom getting soaked through with early dew, and my legs dangling over the edge of the water, as I leaned between the railings and watched. My toe shimmered in the starlight, silvery pale and new. I pressed my knees together hard, and felt the skin give slightly, the blood and veins underneath calling out to each other, moving toward a joining.

Matty's head bobbed up, and his needle teeth shone as he smiled.

"Done?" I asked him. In my pocket, I closed my fingers around the box of cigarettes and pulled it out to slowly unwrap the thin plastic, to fold the silver paper and choose my virgin straw. I tapped it with one fingernail, waiting. A moment later, Ma's head came up alongside Matty's. She was staying in the river, there'd be no three days of rebirth for her. It was better this way. Better to let your dead go than to try hanging on to them.

I took the yellow lighter from my pocket and thought about how quickly the Worme house would burn. By the time the fire department came, I'd be gone. They'd have no idea where to find me. I slipped Ma's cigarette between my lips and closed my eyes. The fire sparked and even through my closed lids I could see the warm redness of it. I breathed in the smoke from my final cigarette. It tasted like acceptance of growing up.

Drowning would hurt, I knew. But first, I had a house to burn down.

I love stories about transformation, and "The Worme Bridge" showcases that. I wrote it for the Short Story Day Africa Water anthology, and was rather shocked and honoured when I got the phone call that the judges had announced my story the winner at the Ake Arts and Book Festival in Nigeria. In this one I play with water and transformation, but also religious resurrection, and the perils of growing up.

This is How We Burn

CALL DOCTOR LOVEGOOD NOW.
HEALER TRADITIONAL MEDICINE.

The ink was blue, fading across the flyer into what might have once been red but was now the pink of discarded Valentine's cards. A rainbow wave of disquiet and superstition. An A5 job lot – 5000 flyers for seven hundred grimy South African rands. Lindela scanned the rest of the flyer, though it was nothing new. Just a distraction. Like the lulling rattle of the wheels against the track. A measure for passing time.

SPELL TO PROTECT YOUR HOUSE MAKE LADY LIKE NEW
HAVE EXTRA-STRONG MALE PART WIN LOTTERY
DESTROY YOUR ENEMY PROTECT FROM SICKNESS SEE
INTO FUTURE BRING LUCK TO FAMILY IMPROVE BUSINESS

They were ubiquitous, these badly-printed flyers. Handed out on roadsides, stuffed into mail boxes, pasted on lamp posts and the sides of trains. Just another 086 number and a list of things that witchcraft would give you.

It wasn't about his penis. He was happy enough with that, and the lottery was a tax on the poor, so Lindela never played, even when he would daydream about what he could do with a million rand. Who were his enemies? Faceless men in the night, with knives and knobkieries. White boys driving white Nissan bakkies, drunk on Castle lager and self-righteousness and fear of some new world order they wouldn't even try to understand.

GET BACK LOST LOVER.

Lindela hunched over on the sweat-damp train seat, and hugged his laptop bag closer to his chest. His charm. His lyre. He was on standby tonight, otherwise he'd have just had left it at the office. Better to not take a risk of getting mugged. But standby paid well, and hey, this was Cape Town, if he did get jumped for his work computer, the company's insurance would cover it.

Tonight he would charm rows of inexplicable code into order, make art from something most people saw as artless. He would see the moon-hare through its journey, sleepless and lost in a glowing labyrinth of his own making. It was better. Better than going clubbing with friends from the Before Times and falling into a mocking underworld, or eating sushi and pretending he cared about stupid uncooked Japanese fish and cold rice. It was better than getting drunk alone or with an audience. It was better than misery.

The train slowed at the stop before his, and the last few people got out of the carriage, leaving Lindela alone with his laptop, and a sleeping woman dressed in demure navies and blacks, still with her gold name badge pinned to her lapel. The book she'd been reading (*The Guernsey Literary and Potato Peel Pie Society*) had fallen against her thigh. She snored softly, and Lindela shifted his laptop onto the seat. Quickly so as not to be caught out for a fool, he stood up to take a photo of the torn flyer pasted above her head. The phone clicked softly, and the image flashed.

It was ridiculous. He didn't need a spell. He didn't believe in witchdoctors and magic. He believed in flat whites at Truth, and wine-soaked book launches at the Book Lounge, Long Street gallery nights, and hashtagged arguments on Twitter.

He tucked the phone back into his pocket, swung the laptop bag to his shoulder, and went to the doors as the trains screeched to another slow halt.

Everyone was waiting for the rains. Summer had burned itself out across the mountains, a raging line of flame that had left a litter of bones, black timber, ash like fallout. People had lost their homes. The ones in the cliff-side mansions had made the news – streaming down the slopes in their silver SUV's, packed with passports and family dogs. The other mountainside homes – the ones no one wanted to see – they were also gone. Whole communities wiped out. People walking barefoot away from their deaths.

But now the mountains were white with ash, clawed with the charcoal sticks of fynbos. Lindela liked to think that under the powdery mantle the fire slept, waiting to return. Just like Lesego, who would also come back one day.

No.

Stupid thinking. Lindela brought the image of the witchdoctor's promises up on his phone and deleted it. Bang. There were better things to trust in. Still, the clouds were creeping in soft as returning cats, and the air smelled like the promise of rain. It sweetened the ragged after-taste of wood ash that still clung to the mountain flanks. Before, Lindela and Lesego had hiked those mountains, stopping to pray and kiss in the rubble of broken buildings, they had left their sweat on old red stones. Under its veil, the mountain still remembered them, Lindela knew.

He would hike this weekend. Do something constructive instead of sitting alone in his room wishing he was dead, wishing for things he could not have. He would walk the old trails and remember happier times.

Until then, he was going to distract himself with a new project. An app for remembering the dead. It would scour the internet for pictures of Lesego, for words he'd said, things he'd liked, little snippets and scratches of web-caught memory, and send them to Lindela. Messages from beyond, Lindela supposed. Morbid, but a way to pretend that Lesego was not gone, not really; he'd merely stepped into some other room.

Sunday came, still dry, but the rain was thick in Lindela's mouth. Ripe and sweet and cold. He tongued the air, let it flow across his palate. His window looked out onto a deep blue darkness just touched with hazy grey and the faint reflected twinkle of the distant lights of Simon's Town. He would leave now before the sun rose, and walk up to the top peak before the wind woke, before the hikers with their over-friendly dogs, before the German tourists in their neat lines and long socks came puffing up the slopes. He would be alone with Lesego and with memories.

He strode up the steps of Peck's Valley as the sun turned the ocean pink, his legs aching with the familiar hike-and-step of climbing the rock stairways. He was alone with the sound of his own breath, with the acrid smell of summer's dead fires. The fire had scarred the land, leaving the bushes little blackened twists of arms in a hellscape. Here and there the burned ground was softened by a valiant spike of greeny-grey. The mountain streams were long dry and there was no sound of birdcalls or softly peeping frogs.

Lindela was almost at the flattened plain at the top of the mountain when he stumbled over the carcass. Smaller than a wallet, round as a stone. The burnt-out carapace of some little tortoise, too slow to outrun death. Lindela slipped it into the side pocket of his rucksack and walked higher, turning onto the trails that would take him right to the wind-buffeted peak, where he could sit on a ledge and watch the whole of False Bay spread out like a blue picnic blanket.

It wasn't just the shell. By the time he reached the peak, Lindela had collected the fragile skull of a tiny bird; a length of bone longer than his finger; and handful of burst and blackened seed cones. He didn't even know why he was collecting them. Memento mori, funereal gifts. One by one they were added to his pockets.

Finally, tucked onto his secluded ledge just below the peak, his feet dangling into space, Lindela pulled out his water bottle and his grisly collection. Dark ash covered his fingertips, coal-black smears crossed his wrists like the marks left by manacles.

What were these things? Reminders? He didn't want them, didn't want to weigh himself down with the dead. Lindela laughed, a painful little self-mockery. As hard as he could, he hurled the offerings into the void. The shell tumbled down the rock face, the sound surprisingly big in the emptiness. The skull and bone followed, and the rising sun turned the distant clouds a fierce gold and pink. He took a mouthful of water, and waited for the rain to come, to wash the sweat and stink from his aching head like a baptism.

It did not.

"Are you alone here?" A woman's voice, crackled like pork fat on the edges. A smoky, salty voice.

Lindela jerked his head up, craned round to look at the woman standing above him, the wind tearing at her mud-daubed hair. "Yes, alone." She didn't seem dangerous. Just a little crazy, some mountain dweller living in crevices, eating stolen food. Her skin was lightened with a mask of white ash and clay, and her eyes stood out blackly in contrast. Lindela got slowly to his feet and scrambled up to the path way. Probably she just wanted to ask him for food or money. It's not like that was unusual here.

The woman stood very tall, Lindela realised when he drew level with her. And the weird lumpy sack she wore was actually the moth-chewed remains of a springbok pelt lashed over one shoulder. Her arms were rich with bracelets of copper and ivory, and when she smiled at him, her teeth were very white and very straight.

"Molweni, Mama. Are you well?" Lindela spoke politely. She looked like something out of the past – a witch-priestess or something. Certainly, not one to offend.

The woman only smiled wider. "So polite, little boy," she said. "Mama? Is that how you greet death?"

She was mad, then. "Death? Sorry, Mama. I must go –"

"Why call me if you can't face me?" She held out a hand to stop him. "You sent for me with the rattle of bones, with empty shells filled with heartache, and now you say you must go?" Her grin stretched, baboon-fanged. "Go where, little boy? Go where?" She spread her arms and the mountains fell away, the blue-grey sky turned to blackness and nothing.

Lindela stumbled back, puffs of white ash rising around him, small brittle things crunching beneath his hiking boots. "I didn't send anything – you're crazy –"

"Not crazy." Her voice dropped and she regarded him for a moment, her wide-set eyes half-closed as if against the glare of a sun that did not penetrate this empty new world. "Next you will tell me you don't believe in magic, that you cast no spells. But, Lindela Ntlotshane, magic doesn't need you to believe in it. The world is bigger than anything you can imagine, and it does not need you."

Lindela swallowed, unable to move. She had called him by name, her voice the tongue-flicker of a serpent against his heart.

"You summoned me for this." She stepped back, fingers beckoning. Out of the darkness a second figure shuffled. Shorter than Lindela, stockier. Half-asleep or dreaming with a vacant expression and eyes like emptied eggshells.

"Lesego!" The name was ripped out of Lindela's throat, tearing its hooks into his oesophagus, catching at his tongue.

The man who had been Lesego in life slowly turned his hollow gaze onto Lindela. His mouth stayed slack. No sound, no cry of recognition.

"What – what's wrong with him?"

"Nothing," said the woman. "Beyond being dead. But you have called for me. You have sung your strange music, and walked the high road into my kingdom, so I will give you a chance to claim him back."

"And how must I do that?" He couldn't look at the woman as he asked, his gaze was pinned to Lesego, too busy memorising the contours of his skull, the curve of his lips, the slight flare of nose of cheekbone of eyebrow. All these collections of artistry that made a human.

She didn't answer.

Lindela had nothing. He'd heard of games of chance against the devil, out-smoking him on a mountain top, or trickery and sleight of hand, but these weren't things he could do. He was only a normal guy who caught the train to work and liked simple things. Who watched the news, and kept his social media profile neat and inoffensive. He wasn't a fiddle-player, a trickster, a poet. He wrote code for Android apps.

Hand trembling, Lindela pulled his phone from his pocket. The last thing he'd done was Instagram a shot of the sunrise, but there were other things there – a rough and still-buggy version of his little private project. He flicked the screen with his thumb, and called up the photo of Lesego. He was smiling, shy and nervous in that picture, arms around his mother's neck, bending over her. Too sweet for his own good. Lindela coughed, surprised by the pain of that remembered day, and handed the phone over to death.

She watched for a while, watched what Lindela knew would be an onslaught of images, of lines taken out of context from Tumblr posts and Facebook statuses. Tweets from five years ago, pictures of Lesego alone, Lesego at work, with his ageing mother, with their friends, with his sister, with Lindela.

Death stared for a long time, unmoved. Finally, she handed the phone back with a casual toss.

Lindela caught it, and the phone froze just as one image was ghosting into another. "Memories," he said, not looking up. "That's all you've left me of him, and it's not enough."

"I would like to tell you my heart has been moved, but I've met finer poets than you who couldn't bring me to tears."

Despair sunk through his flesh, making him feel heavy and useless. Lindela looked away from the ghosting image, back to her face.

"And even if I were moved, it wouldn't matter. I have fed your

Lesego three white maize kernels. I have set my teeth in him. He can no more return to the living world than I can become the Queen of the Sun."

"Then why –" He wanted to say – *why toy with me, why mock me, why offer so cruelly*? But Lindela shut his mouth instead. Who was he to argue with death?

"Because, little boy, I think you can do something for me, and in exchange I will let you visit here, I will let you stay for as long as the rains fall, and Lesego will remember you." She shrugged, and the skin around her shoulders rippled like it had been filled with the dreams of snakes.

"Yes."

"Yes?" Her black eyes glittered. "You don't even know what I want from you."

"It doesn't matter." Lindela stepped forward to touch the hand of the man he had once known and loved, who he still did. Lesego's fingers were cold but under that coldness, Lindela could detect a pulse, a flicker. A banked coal of warmth. He would breathe it awake. His lover's eyes moved and there was a moment of recognition. The dead mask became Lesego's face truly. His mouth moved, whispering the secret language of warm sheets and tongues of fire.

Lindela could already taste their kisses, could feel the warmth of their meeting. "Tell me," he said softly, "and I'll do it."

The winter had passed in veils of mist and rain, seeding the flanks of the mountains with new life. Spring was almost over, tender and still softly damp. The summer heat was blowing in, a dry tongue licking the new grasses and recovering fynbos.

Lindela stood on the sea-side window of his apartment, watching the blue sky, the people walking on the street below – going into the library, to the grimy cafe-market to buy fishing tackle and overpriced milk. He watched the men and women drinking their cold beers and eating greasy fish and chips in the little restaurant across the street. No rain clouds drifted overhead, casting shadows across their faces. To the east he could spot the bright sails of the kite-surfers dancing in the stiff winds. So normal and human, and so utterly strange to him now. He was back from death, flushed full with love and happiness. He'd had his season. But now the rains were over and it was time to pay the price he would have to pay every dry summer from now on. His exchange, his offering of sacrifices. The thousands of little deaths she fed on.

Not this weekend, not the next, but in a month or so he would go hiking. He would choose a dead bright day, wind-whipped and ready, cheap plastic lighter in his pocket. Under an empty sky he would walk alone until he found a dry place gone crackly with old growth, and he would pay her price. Until then.... Lindela thumbed on his phone and flicked the little avatar of Lesego's face. Until the fires started and until they burned themselves out to bone ash and blackened grit, he would remember.

Set in Muizenberg again, on the mountainsides where I would regularly walk my dogs. This was an Orpheus story that went wrong. It was inspired by the terrible fires that rage every year on Muizenberg's mountains, causing much destruction and death. It was me wondering why people set fires, and coming up with this.

A Green Silk Dress and a Wedding-Death

Héloise Oudejan lived by a cursed river that bled into a black ocean. She'd grown up in a two-room cottage that smelled of fish scales and outdoor latrines, webby with spider silk and ghosts. The Oudejan house stood at the far end of Jitter Lane, squashed side to side with eleven other same-faced fisher-cottages; two rooms and a stone hearth, peeling plaster, dripping eaves. Héloise knew the feel of damp cold on the walls and underfoot. It was the river pushing its way up through thick red clay, moving bones, rearranging the dead so that Oma would have to poke the fire high and mutter invocations against restless spirits.

She'd been doing just that when Héloise left for work: Oma bent over the fire, speaking to the dead in a dead language, while Héloise's little brother Gwil snored in Oma's bed.

Gwil was the reason Héloise got up every morning. Why today, like every day, she'd dressed in her mended clothes and stumbled through the dark, remembering her way along the rutted path that led toward town and the docks. Héloise lived life through a veil of blurs and shadows, everything fuzzy at the edges and incomplete. Only if she held something close could she see the intricate wonder of it in perfect detail. Her impression of the world was formed in microscopic snatches, piecemeal. She recognized one person from another by the way they walked, and if she stuck her nose into a book she could parse a sentence word by slow word, but that was the best of it.

On her first day of school she'd been placed at the back of the class and forgotten. Héloise had never been able to read the scrawled chalk on the pale green of the blackboards, but she'd known better than to make a fuss. Making a fuss didn't get you nowhere except maybe dead.

Instead, Héloise had learned to listen.

She listened all the way to work, to the sound of the foghorns and the waves, and the slow drone of the trucks taking goods inland. When she got to the docks, she would listen to the gossip and the news and the stories, and tuck the knowledge away. If she listened hard enough, Héloise had found that she could see the shape of things, know which way the world was turning.

Now she had a job in the harbour, where being shortsighted didn't make a difference. She'd left school at sixteen and learned to scale and gut fish so that Gwil always had food, and wouldn't grow up pinched and bitter.

Héloise's hands were always cold and stained. Her hair stank of rotten seaweed no matter how often she washed it, and the smell crept into her clothes and skin, became a part of her.

Back when she'd been knee-high to a toad, and before Mama'd gone and got herself killed, Héloise believed that the world could be better. That one day she'd wear new dresses instead of charity rags, that she'd wake up and the world would have drawn into focus, suddenly clear and crisp. She would know the whole of things and not just the parts she could examine in close-up.

A car rattled past her and Héloise recognised it by the hiccupping skip of the engine. It was Ou Tien on his own way down to meet his son's boat.

"Thanks," she said to the fumes. She was practical enough to know that her boss wouldn't bother to offer her a lift. Didn't mean she had to like it.

Oma always said, "Wishing for sweeter makes you sour," which Héloise had taken to mean, "Shut up and stop your whining." And it was true that wanting what you couldn't have only turned a heart bitter. Heloise had seen that with her own mother, so she'd stopped bothering and made the best of the good that fell confetti-small into her life.

The sun was just silvering the sea by the time Héloise reached the docks. Atikka had got there before her and was bringing in the baskets of fresh-caught fish. Atikka was one piece of confetti – an almost-friend. Like Héloise, she spent her mornings scaling and gutting fish, but she was a little younger, a little fatter, a little more loved. Despite this, she would spend the morning working alongside Héloise, sighing deeply, wrapped in a constant shroud of love-sick misery.

The morning passed in the slap of wet fish against the slick cobbles, the spill of guts, the shower of scales, and always, as a counterpoint to the glassy gasping of the fish, Atikka's ever-lengthening sighs.

The sky had turned a deep and endless blue, the kind most conducive to stretching out bare legs under a baking sun and daydreaming in mindless productivity. The men had offloaded their catches and the girls prepared them for market, while the older women sold fish and molluscs to housewives and merchants. The chatter and buzz of the dock markets were a soothing, familiar pattern. Héloise didn't need to see it to know. The hum was regular. It spoke of constancy and purpose. The mundane rhythm of it was a comforting, boring story; far from curses and ghosts, and families full of secrets.

Atikka, sweat frizzing her hair and staining the armpits of her bleached sundress, set down her blade. A half-scaled fish lay across her brown legs like a dead baby. She looked mournfully down at it and sighed for the hundredth time.

"Who are you mooning over now?" Héloise asked, finally defeated. It was a boy. Because it was always a boy. Listening to Atikka talk about her doomed romances was part of the price of friendship.

"Jutien," Atikka said. "He keeps walking past."

Jutien was the son of the boss. A fisherboy nearing manhood who spent all his nights out on the water and still somehow found the time and energy to stroll through the day markets to look at the girls. He called it 'Inspections' and said he liked to keep an eye on the stalls, but no girl was stupid enough to fall for it, even though all the talk was of how handsome he was, and about his wicked smile.

He had a voice that trickled into Héloise's ears like warmed syrup. Even if she didn't like Jutien much, Héloise still enjoyed the sound of him.

"I think he's looking at me," Atikka said.

"He's not," snapped Héloise as she ran her blade down the length of a large fish. The scales fell in a dry patter of tarnished silver. The lumpy and uneven stones of the harbour market were littered with scales that dulled and turned to trash as soon as they landed. Just like the girls on Fish Lane, really, Héloise thought. She didn't want Atikka believing Jutien was worth mooning over, not when the girl still had a scrap of dreaming to her. Men like Jutien threw a mantle of charm over themselves to hide their broken knuckles and bruised fists.

Héloise and Atikka worked for Jutien's father, which meant both men acted as though they owned the girls. They could speak to them any way they pleased, tell them to work longer, or send them home after a bad catch without pay. Jutien once had Héloise up against a brick wall in the small lanes about a year ago, back when she'd thought he was pretty and that sweet talk was a good enough substitute for affection. He'd kissed her in a way that made her feel she was choking to death, before he'd turned her around and pressed her against the wall. She remembered the damp scratch of brick, the smell of clay and moss and salt, the sharp suddenness of copper and come. He'd been, if not her first, certainly the first she'd thought herself almost caring for, and with the grunting thrust and jab of his exertions had come to the realization that, once again, this was all she was going to get.

After that, she never went out of her way to catch any boy's eye. Not because there was no fun to be had, but because it all felt pointless, and all the little rush got you was a fat belly and more laundry and more mouths crying at you, and less food to go around.

And Atikka, silly and plump and loved as she was, didn't deserve that as a future.

"Jutien looks at everyone like that – he'll take any girl who's willing." Héloise hadn't meant to be quite so sharp toward her little almost-friend. After all, Atikka was still a butterbrain, butterball, butterheart. Not that Héloise believed in saving people from themselves, but people talked. Atikka could go follow her heart and find it scraped raw, split open, or Héloise could talk instead of listening.

Truth was, Héloise was better at the other. She'd never learned to use words carefully.

Her cut had been too sharp, too pointed, and little butterball Atikka turned nasty. "Oh will he?" she said sourly, all sighs puffed away by hot anger. "That's not what *I* heard."

"Oh, that's right? What did you hear?" Héloise scraped faster, fiercer, and flung the cleaned fish into its basket with the others.

"You're jealous." Atikka had abandoned her work.

Héloise kept her neck bowed, listening, not looking. Her hands were still moving, slicing heads and tails clean so that Jutien's father could sell the scraps to poor wives and cheap kitchens.

Jealous? There was a thing. Héloise would have laughed, but Atikka was talking again.

"Jealous because you want him and he won't touch you."

The gutted fish stared at her with wide, dry, condemning eyes, their bellies flopped open palely, the thin pinkness of their blood just staining the almost translucent flesh. Héloise pushed the point of her blade against one round eye and wished she didn't have to listen to the things people said about her.

"Lissa down our way says he won't touch you because you're not worth the splitting open, you're such a fish-stinking, salt-water bitch."

Salt-water bitch. Not the first time Héloise had heard that levelled at her. She recalled the same words from her father, spat at her mother after another night of drinking. A repeated story, with the same mean little ending.

She walked home the long way, not wanting to go straight from bleeding cold fingers that never stopped stinging to Gwil's snot-nose and Oma's sour, collapsed face; bitter and aged and tired, the smell of old deaths hidden.

She took the narrow dry path that tacked through the fields past the school she no longer went to, toward the river.

The river was dark and brackish and wide as an empty future. Now and again, fishermen staked nets when there was a silverside spawning run, but mostly they left the estuary waters to itself. In winter, Héloise came and gathered bundles of reeds, and borrowed Uncle Kavanei's curved thatching hook to fix the house roof, but otherwise she, too, stayed away.

There were things living in the river, things that were best left undisturbed. People didn't say what, exactly, but she got the impression from their tone and whispers that they were bad things. Héloise figured that since she was also a bad thing, it really wouldn't make much difference if she sat on the riverbank and let her bare feet hang in the gently swirling water. The river was stained red as tea, but that was from tree roots and tannins, she knew. Local legend said the river flowed bloody once a month, like a woman, unclean and deadly, but it was just more bullshit the people in the fishing town made up because their lives were so small and stupid.

The water was cool, soothing aches from her feet, and the sun was low and hot, warming her thighs and knees, reddening them a little. Tomorrow she'd be tanned olive as a stick. That was one nice thing about having sallow skin. She didn't burn, just turned a deep golden brown that rich girls tried to fake with powders and sprays.

Héloise looked around. The place was deserted, screened by little gnarled bushes with small, bright leaves. The birds called their same songs, the water rushed and slapped, but there was no swish of people moving through the grasses, or the suck of muddied footsteps. Satisfied that she was alone and unseen, she hiked her skirt up so that her legs could tan all the way to her panty line, and pulled off her top to reveal a rather saggy grey bra with the elastic long-since shot. It was the closest she'd get to a bikini tan.

The sun felt like a large warm hand that pressed gently against her back, that smoothed its fingertips down her neck and massaged the ache from her temples. She closed her eyes and lost herself in the bright red and orange burst of sun on closed lids, in the trickle of water and birdsong, and the faraway drone and call of the village traffic.

It felt, for a moment, good. And that was okay, too. That was the thing about everyone running around looking for some level of good they couldn't reach instead of just enjoying the good that they could. The problem with the world, Héloise thought. She was smarter than the rest of them, in this much at least. Let them call her names; let Jutien and Atikka and the people like them live their narrow lives.

What did it matter? You could listen but it didn't mean you had to believe. That's what Mama had done. Believed all the things people said, and what had that got her in the end?

Not much of nothing.

Not much of a story to pass on.

Héloise was half-dozing, the sun sinking low, its caresses growing colder and more distant like a lover working out how to leave quietly, when she heard the splash. She was used to the bright, high slap of a fish leaping from the water, but this was bigger, a sound of shift and change, and Héloise opened her eyes to see the silver blur of a fish, big as woman's thigh, leap from the bloodied waters and hang in midair, a moment suspended out of time.

Héloise stared at the fish, and the fish's bulging pearl-and-black eye stared at her.

Springer, she thought. But it couldn't be. Not that big.

The fish moved, shimmered, and in its place stood a black-and-pearl-eyed boy. No, a man, or some creature in a state between the two. He was wearing bright armour, metal scales overlapping, and he held a long, thin spear, white and sharp as splintered bone. His hair was sea-spray and the glint on the water. And that was all Héloise could make from her blurred and fragmentary world.

She stayed motionless, half in amazement and half in shame that she was sitting on a riverbank in old underwear with her short skirt rolled up past her panty line. Just another docks-girl, easy. A salt-water bitch. An unexpected surge of hate for men like Jutien rolled through her, hot and raw.

But the fish-mail boy didn't notice her. He waded through the red water, thrusting his spear to impale bright, writhing fish. When he pulled the first from his spear and brought it to his face, Héloise thought he was going to eat it raw. Instead, he kissed the fish and set it free, blood meeting red river water. He did this again and again, and Héloise sat still, frozen, as dusk fell, and her vision grew worse until all she could see was the pale flick of hair and fish, of scale and spear.

And then he was gone.

She breathed out slowly, shivering, her skin goosefleshed. Carefully, every movement stiff from the cold and from sitting too long, Héloise rolled her skirt down and pulled her top back on. Oma and Gwil would be waiting.

Heloise trailed home in the green light of almost-evening and wondered what she had just seen. Not human, for sure. A river spirit, perhaps? But he hadn't looked right for their river. A river spirit here should be thick and old, bloated with silt and dyed crimson and brown.

Perhaps, like a salmon, he was a sea-thing spawned in fresh water. An ocean spirit. That's why she'd never seen him before. He was moving downriver, closer to the ocean.

Or perhaps he was nothing, and she'd been dreaming in the late-day sun, seeing things that weren't there. After all, her vision was never to be trusted. Héloise shook her head and trudged through the stretching darkness.

The first sign that the water spirit had been more than nothing was the fish.

Jutien dumped his catch at Héloise's and Atikka's feet. "Would you fucking look at this!" he yelled, as though the catch was their fault.

Atikka scrabbled back, panting. "Oh, that's hideous!"

Unable to see the exact problem, Héloise leaned forward to pull the nearest fish from the wide basket. The first fish looked fine until inspected close-up, as did the second. The third was a monstrosity. It had once been a yellowmouth, but now it was a knot of twisted flesh with tails sprouting where its eyes should have been, and a row of dully staring round eyes along its side, following the swim-line. Héloise shuddered and ran a fingertip lightly along its broad scales. They felt strangely slimy, soft. The fish gasped, still almost alive, and Héloise looked into a mouth filled with another head, a tiny screaming row of teeth within teeth. She tossed the fish down. "How many?"

Jutien kicked the basket with the side of his foot, then shoved his hands in his pockets. "More than half the catch."

That was unusual. Sports turned up now and again, but never in such numbers. "Why didn't you throw them back?"

"And have them breeding? Nah, fuck, we'll grind this lot up and sell it to the pig and fowl merchants for feed." He grinned. "You girls can sort 'em for me."

"Ugh, Jutien, no..." Atikka said. "What if I catch something from them?"

"I'll do it," Héloise said. She felt vaguely sorry for the fish. They hadn't asked to be born hideous and strange.

The week was filled with monstrosities. Every catch was more gruesome than the last, the tortured fish more misshapen, their deformities reaching extremes that even Héloise found disturbing.

"Why?" she asked Atikka one day. Their brief standoff was over, Atikka's sulking silence broken by the need to share her life with someone, even if that someone was Héloise.

"What's happened? Has anyone said anything about what might have caused it?" A toxic spill, a bacteria bloom... even a sudden storm that had washed monsters up from the deep. But Héloise had heard nothing.

"It's a curse," said Atikka.

Héloise thought of the fish-mail boy kissing the fish before setting them back in the water. But those had been river fish, not ocean fish. *Rivers flow to the sea.* The thought turned her stomach. Had the water spirit set some vengeful curse into the seas? *Why would he?* she wondered as she chopped the deformed fish, piling them up into piles of squarish chunks. These were going to be sent to the farmers. No one was happy about it. The feed sold cheap – too cheap – and people were swearing up and down that now the eggs they bought tasted like fish. Soon, they would have to sell the discards as fertilizer. Cheap-cheap.

Atikka or Héloise would be fired. There wasn't money enough to pay two girls. Her knife landed with a solid *thunk*. Not Atikka. She was still waiting to be captured, falling for Jutien's mulberry words, sweet and tart-black.

It would be Héloise. She drew in a deep breath and chopped faster.

"Jutien says," said Atikka, "that there's a story about this."

"Is there now." There were always stories. Héloise settled in to listen to them, to add them to her store.

"Yeah, going back all the way to when the Ilin lived here."

The Ilin who were mostly gone, wiped out by disease and betrayal and interbreeding with the Kari, who had come sweeping in from the eastern reaches, toward the sea.

"Tell me this story," said Héloise.

"Oh, I don't know it. Superstitious Ilin nonsense from upriver. Something about how the spirit is angry because no one gives him sacrifices any more." Atikka set down her own blade and stretched her arms high over her head, fingers linked. "My back is killing me. You know the kind of things."

"What things? Why would I know?"

"Ugh, come on. Your oma's mostly Ilin, I heard. You've got a little of their look, you know."

"No." Héloise stabbed her knifepoint down into her chopping board. "I don't. Anyway, I'm done here. I'll just take this basket up to Ou Tien and then I'm off."

"Mmm." Atikka looked away. "I'll wait for Jutien, he said he'd give me a lift home."

Héloise bit her lips so that she wouldn't let her exasperation stream out of her. "Watch yourself," was all she said, and Atikka scowled.

"Tell me," Héloise said to Oma, while she cracked long green beans into a chipped bowl, the sweet green pop satisfying as breaking a neck, "about the river spirits of the Ilin."

Oma snorted imperiously; an empress in ashes at the stove. She was frying mustard seeds and crushed garlic, the water pot frothing and ready for the green beans to blanch. Green beans and mutant fish that

Héloise bought when none of the other workers could see her, Jutien smirking as he sold her pig food. "You don't want to hear that rubbish," Oma said, in a way that only made Héloise want to more.

Mama had been Ilin, too. It was only Papa who had snagged her to civilization, beaten his salt-water bitch sound and sweet, then killed her so she would learn not to talk back. Their bones were under the hearthstones. Héloise knew this because she had helped Oma boil the meat from their bodies. They had fed the flesh and broth to that year's pig, fat and stinking at the bottom of the garden. The bones had gone under the hearth, under iron to keep the ghosts quiet. Only Oma and Héloise knew this. Little Gwil was deaf and blind to truth, innocent and selfish with it.

Oma had killed Papa with the iron skillet, then stitched his mouth closed with fishhooks so that his ghost could never talk. The iron stopped him from roaming, and Oma sung to him in Ilinish to lull him asleep.

The village only knew that Mama had run away, leaving her children – just like any no-good Ilin woman, useless slattern, barbarian witch – and Papa had gone off to bring her back.

No one asked questions.

"I want to hear the stories."

Héloise tipped the beans into the boiling water and the bubbles subsided. "There's a river spirit that Mama used to talk about." She did not say she'd seen it.

Oma looked over to where Gwil was bashing blocks of wood together, making them *brrrm* like cars. "What do you know about your mother?"

Héloise shrugged. "Nothing. She was full-blood, but you and her both lied and said she wasn't. She was born in Cressid, not here, and you came down to join her after the war, in the seventies." Such a sad litany of a life. Héloise could remember little else. Her mother had always struck her as useless. A little rabbit, a frightened, weak, and pathetic thing, cringing from Papa but never running away. She remembered the smell of her breath at night, cheesy-sour with milk-beer, her eyes dark and wide and drugged. Too skinny, bruised. She would forget to wash and the flies sang hymns about her hair, waiting for her to die. She had been a ghost before Papa beat her to death.

There was one good memory only. So bleary and blurry that

Héloise thought it less a memory and more a hopeful dream, a child's wish to make magic from the terrifyingly ordinary.

A green dress.

A silk dress.

A water dress.

Her mother had never worn it, but in Héloise's dream she had unrolled it and held it up to her shoulders, where it flowed down her body like ice-black water, the shadows dark as hidden pools, the green frost of sea storms, of rapids and rills. Her mother had danced, holding the dress to her chest, and for that moment, Mama was beautiful.

A dream too lovely for this cold, musty house where the corners were held together by mouse droppings and dust-hares.

"Your mother was never meant to marry Petit Alessand," Oma said. "She was already spoken for."

"Oh." Héloise took the pot from the stove and drained the beans before handing them to Oma, who swept them deftly into the spiced oil. This was something she'd not heard before. "She was betrothed?"

"No." Oma stirred, her eyes on the food and not on Héloise, but Héloise knew this to be an excuse, an avoidance. Oma could make fish and beans with her eyes bound in black silk. "She was a sacrifice. We understood, even if we did not like it. There are rites and truths older than the Kari will ever understand. Every fifty years, the river needs its sacrifice. Always the most beautiful of our people, young and sweet as a veal-collop. Sometimes a young man, sometimes a maiden. It did not matter. Whoever they were, they were given to the water."

It sounded... barbarous. Unbelievable. It sounded like the things the Kari said about the Ilin. Child sacrifice, evil. Héloise didn't want to hear the rest of the story.

"We dressed her in silk and sorrow," said Oma, "and tied her wrists and ankles with stones that rang like bells; we garlanded her with lily buds and pondweed, and carried her on a stretcher made from young boughs skinned white, the bark burned for incense, the wood smelling sweet and new." She spoke as though the city outside had fallen away, and eyes glowed like lamps in the story-light, ears were pricked.

Héloise hugged herself, and listened.

"She should have drowned. She should have been taken to the water spirit's city, to be his lover in the deep." Oma dropped her head and the song fell out of her voice, leaving it cracked and old again.

"Instead, Petit Alessand came and rescued her. Took her away from her death and gave her this life instead." She sighed deep and low. "So we suffer."

It was bullshit. Of course it was. Made-up Ilin nonsense that Mama had brought with her downriver. Still. "What happens if the sacrifice isn't given?"

"Who knows?" Oma said, and tipped the flesh of warped fish onto the dinner plates. "Come. Eat."

It was Jutien who called the hunt together. On a night when the moon was full and fat and hung between the cape's peaks like a ripe fruit waiting for fingers to reach up and tug it free, he gathered the young men of Derleth village and led them up the blood river, with their long nets, with their spears and their hooks. They went with spells older than their cities and their cars, with long nets of knotted kelp, with spears of black alder, with hooks of moon-kissed silver.

They caught him.

It.

They caught the river spirit as if he were a fish, froth-finned, scale-armoured, mouth gasping, gill-flared. A deep-thing.

Héloise heard their whooping and shouting from the cottage, in dreams, and turned over in her sleep, dampening the pillowcase with tears she would not remember in the morning.

"What's going on?" Héloise sauntered over to Ou Tien's stall, where Atikka was already standing, her hands by her sides, her knives waiting to be picked up. A vast crowd jostled about the market, the sky teeming with gulls. Too busy, even for morning. And the air smelled wrong. It was garlanded with woodsmoke and the pungent reek of milk-beer. "Was there a party last night or something?" Typical if there had been, and her not invited. Fuck, who cared? The men would have ignored her until they were drunk; only then, if they hadn't found a girl to pair off with, would they have pressed her against a wall and pawed at her tits like slobbering imbecile babies.

She could live without an invitation to Kari fun.

"No." Atikka turned to face her, and Héloise squinted, trying to read some expression through the blur of eyes and mouth. "They caught it."

"Caught what?" But Héloise's stomach filled with river pebbles, cold and black. Eels twisted through her intestines.

"The river spirit. There really was one." Atikka's voice had grown childish in her excitement. She sounded like a brat at a party, waiting for the magician to come fool her with doves and flowers. "We can't see it right now. Jutien is charging two shills a look, but he said he'd show me after work. Free, yanno?" She faltered at Héloise's silence. "I'll ask if you can look, too. I'm sure he won't mind."

"It's still alive?" Héloise asked softly. It couldn't be the fish-creature she'd seen leaping from the river. The white-maned man with his pearl-and-black eyes. He had been magical, beautiful. Even Jutien and his people couldn't capture magic and slave it for amusement.

"Uh-huh." Atikka nodded. "They're keeping it in a tank."

"Oi!"

Both girls started at the deep shout, as Ou Tien lumbered into view. "I don't pay you chits to stand about gossiping – You're not haggard fish wives yet. Get to work!"

The day passed like every other day that had gone before, only, Héloise noticed, there were fewer of the malformed fish. Already, the curse was broken. And streams of people swished past her, their feet tapping as they went to pay to see Jutien's monster, his fish-thing from the deep. "Hideous," they shrieked to each other as they left. "Gods, did you see it!" Though of course they had all seen it. They had stood together under the darkened tent Jutien had set up and stared at their nightmares, the impossible made mundane.

"It's a trick," a mustachioed man was telling his beldame as they walked past, trying not to slip on intestines and scales and gull shit. "Some poor deformed boy they've paid to hold his breath and wear outlandish costumes."

"Of course," said the woman. "Hair dye, glue, sequins." She skipped over a raised cobble and splashed muck against Héloise's legs. "Ridiculous, really. That we would fall for superstitious Ilin nonsense."

"We are educated," agreed the man, and Héloise concentrated on gutting fish and not stabbing him in his broad, sweaty back.

When darkness fell in swathes of indigo and orange, in showers of comet dust and echoed streetlights, Jutien took Atikka to see his catch.

"And Hel?" she asked.

Jutien looked at Héloise with a dismissive grunt but said neither yes nor no, so Héloise followed them to the tent. It was small, a little sideshow thing propped up on wooden poles and hammered into place with steel pegs. Red rocks marbled with white held down the edges of the tent walls to stop them flapping in the sea winds. Inside, the light was cold and white and weak from the LED lamps the fishermen took with them at night. The tank sat in the middle. Someone's old, discarded fish tank, the corners stained with algae, the rubber-glue seals limned glow-blue, a fine crack in one corner. It was a big tank for fish, but a small one for a man.

"Dear gods," said Atikka in a low, breathy voice. "Is it real?" She pressed her palm to the glass and the shadowed shape moved, slurring the waters.

"Real as I am," said Jutien. "And ten times as ugly."

"You're not ugly," Atikka said, and the two began a lumbering flirtation.

Héloise ignored them and let the soft glow of the tank pull her forward. She drifted through the dusk-dark, eddies of cold air tugging her to the shallow shadows. She echoed Atikka's touch, fingers and palm to cold glass. Inside, the spirit stared back at her, pearl and black, his white hair wreathed about him. Incense smoke underwater, milk blooming in tea.

Every face Héloise had ever seen was blurred beautiful, and the water spirit was no exception. He was carved smooth by her disability, ugliness rendered clean in plain, broad strokes.

In her head, a man's voice whispered, *Sidonie.*

Héloise drew back, shivering.

Sidonie. You owe me, the voice said. *A green silk dress and a wedding-death, but I'll take the freedom. A fair trade.* It laughed.

Héloise ran away, not caring that Atikka called after her, or that Jutien laughed as cruel and cold as the voice in her head.

Freedom for death wasn't much of a trade. Héloise told herself she should forget about curses and water spirits and green dresses. Mama was long-dead-and-buried, and Héloise didn't owe the spirit anything. The mother's debts were not the daughter's.

The thought stayed in her head, endless as a circle. After all, it wasn't every day river spirits spoke to her. It changed the story.

"Did Mama have a dress?" Héloise asked. Gwil was sick and Oma had been carrying him about all day, trying to soak his fever heat down with cold compresses. Now Héloise cradled his heavy, sweaty body against her chest, cooing and rocking him even though he was no longer a baby.

"She had enough dresses," Oma said. There was no cheap fish left. She was cooking rice gruel with the last tomatoes and cabbage and green peppers from the garden.

"This one was beautiful, though," Héloise said. "It was made of silk, and gr –"

"Your Papa burned it," snapped Oma. "Go ask next door if you can borrow some milk."

She left Gwil crying and went to beg a cup of milk from their neighbour, who gave it to her only out of a wretched pity born of facing the same long road downward. Héloise carried the milk back, and did not cry. Instead, she wondered what a river spirit would give her if she fulfilled her mother's sacrifice.

Sure, freedom for death mightn't be a good trade. But freedom for freedom? That was a better one.

Héloise had to wait for Gwil and Oma to fall asleep before she could go sneaking to Oma's bed, to pull out from under it the bashed and rusted tin chest that had once held anything of value. It scratched against the floor, and Oma muttered in her sleep, but did not wake as Héloise carefully carried it to the other end of the house.

There was no key. Or rather, there was, but Oma wore it around her neck on a piece of dirty string, and Héloise had no intention of trusting her luck that far. Instead, she used one of the pins from her hair and wiggled and wriggled it until the tiny levers clicked into place and she could swing the lid up. It groaned on ungreased hinges, sounding like Papa waking from a hangover so bad he wished for death.

Inside were papers. Papers of birth, old letters, money from another country long gone. There was a small blue vase made of milky glass that Héloise vaguely remembered seeing last when she was no older than Gwil was now. She touched it gently, found the seam where it had been inexpertly glued back together, was bitten by the ragged chip on its fluted lip. The papers rustled at her, the sound of leaves burning, and she pushed them aside.

The dress lay at the bottom, sunk down beneath the layers to settle cold as silt, slick between Héloise's fingers. She drew it out slowly and closed the tin box.

It was still dark when she reached the emptied market. The steel bones of the stalls broke the space into an architectural skeleton of squared-off ribs and narrow femurs. The tent stood in the middle, lights glowing around it, a guard at the front. He was one of Jutien's crowd, a boy-man with thick red hair and wide lips. August would one day be almost handsome in a raw and powerful way, but for now he was thick-fingered and broad-cheeked and hollow-ribbed with growing.

Héloise stripped in the shadows, dropping her grey panties and stretched-out bra into a puddle of ugliness, then reached upward and let the silk fall down her body, a gliding wave that left her teeth chattering, her skin prickled with gooseflesh. The dress made her breath steam the air, her hands and feet go numb with pain.

Dressed for her mother's wedding-death, Héloise went to the guard.

"You're not meant to be here," August said. "Agh, it's only you. What do you want?"

"To see the monster."

"Ha, like I'm going to let you go in for free. Five shills."

"Jutien's only charging two."

August leaned on his wooden staff and laughed. The white lanterns threw whiplash stripes across his face "So? I'm not Jutien."

"I don't have any money." Héloise held herself in her river-water dress and waited for heat to come back to her, but instead she grew colder. She could smell salt and brackish stink, rotting fish, the pungent black reek of trapped mud and debris. It lifted from her skin in waves.

"Yeah. Didn't think so."

Héloise waited for him to come to his conclusion, breathing in slow relief when he smiled sly and said, "But I heard things from Jutien about you..."

The tent flap fell closed behind her. There were no lamps lit now, and it took a few moments for her sight to adapt to the starless dark. She could hear the bubble and hum of the pumps, the soft, slow splash of moving water.

Sidonie.

Héloise shook her head. "I'm not her."

You're wearing her dress.

"I'm wearing *my* dress." Naked beneath the silk, August's seed running down her legs. "I'm here to set you free." She could do it. There were stones littered around the tent. It had been simple to pick one up once August was dreamy-satisfied and hide it in the folds of her skirt. She lifted her fist, the stone pointed like a dagger. She was strong. One good blow. "And we're not far from the sea. You can run, yes?"

There was no answer, but the shadow in the water moved. A nod, Héloise thought, from the way his white hair curled and streamed.

"But I won't set you free," she whispered. "Not even for her. Her debts are not mine."

The river spirit waited.

"What happens to the sacrifices?" she asked. Those girls and boys from a country she'd never seen. Héloise knew all about sacrifices. Mama had withered away before she died, but she'd sacrificed herself anyway, stayed with Petit Alessand so that her children would have a father. Or something. Perhaps it would have been better to go to a faster death. "When you drown them?"

It cocked its head. *What do you think?*

"Death, I suppose."

And after that? The water spirit sounded curious. *Do you believe death is all there is for humans?*

"Guess I'll find out." She shrugged. "Today, or some other day."

The spirit laughed soundlessly in the water, bell-ringing in her head. So loud her temples throbbed and Héloise winced. "You will give me more than death," she said when the chime faded, "or I'll leave you here. Jutien will get bored of you, eventually. The town will stop paying to see how ugly you are, and you'll cost Jutien more to keep than you're worth. Lights, pumps, a guard on duty." She waved her free hand at the small, enclosed space. "What happens when Jutien gets bored of you? He caught you, and he always gets bored of the things he catches."

You tell me. The voice managed to sound sulky, almost human.

"He will cut your head from your shoulders and give you to me. I will gut you. I will slide a knife under your scales and they will litter the cobbles. Jutien will take your broken body away in a basket. He will feed your flesh through a grinder and sell you to pig farmers."

The spirit stared. *Fine. We will make a bargain, Sidonie.*

"Not Sidonie." Héloise swallowed. "She's dead. You get me

instead. Now, how do I keep you to a promise?"

The spirit drifted closer to the tank glass, and Héloise stepped forward to meet it. She could always see too much when she was close, the pores of skin, the fine wrinkles, the tiny scabs and sores that went unnoticed by others. No big picture for Héloise, just innumerable fine details.

The spirit's eyes were shifting rings of silver and pearl and ebony, round-pupiled and unblinking; his scales were a rainbow sheen, each so small that they could only be seen by Héloise. *There is no promise, Sidonie. There is only trust. My name is Sil e Catthia, and I will not drown a willing spouse.*

It was not quite the bargain Héloise had wanted but it was better than staying in a two-room cottage, turning sour and growing old, working for Jutien, scaling fish and eating cabbage soup. It was better than one day falling into a marriage because there was nowhere else to go. Better than broken bones and being buried under a hearth. It was better than failing forever.

Instead of a slow trudge to death, it was an unexpected step sideways. "So the rest weren't willing, then?"

Héloise listened for an answer that only she could hear.

"Oi, how long you gonna be in there?" August called from outside the tent. "You said five minutes."

"Tell me," Héloise whispered, fiercely.

Sil shook his head. Trust.

Trust the word of a monster. Héloise closed her eyes for a moment. She knew what real monsters were. Men like Petit Alessand and Jutien, and August. Small, petty monsters who broke women slowly with words and fists and sneers. Who used them up and discarded them when they were bent and shrivelled.

Here she stood, dressed to meet a monster out of stories. At least this way, maybe she would become bigger than just half-blind Héloise Oudejan who lived at the end of Jitter Lane. Her name would be a warning told to children. *Don't do this. Don't wish for more. Know your place.*

And somewhere, someone would listen to the story that lay under the warning. The story that whispered, *But she did not die old and broken; she became queen of the deep; she became cold and clean as a curse, and now when the market boys call her a salt-water bitch, you can see the whites of their eyes.*

"My name is Héloise a Sidonie, and I will not gut a willing spouse."

She raised the stone and smashed it hard as she could against the glass, at the weakest point. The side shattered and fell with a massive crash, the water falling in a shower of brokenness. She dropped the stone and grabbed blindly, felt the slick fish-skin under her palm and closed her fingers. "Run!"

He did not drown her, though the water was so cold, so salty, so raging, so black that Héloise thought perhaps it didn't matter. She choked on her fear as Sil pulled her down; she choked on his kiss until she grew bold enough to return it. He tasted of fresh white mussels, like the sea.

They went deeper, far from where the estuary spilled red water and broken vegetation into the ocean. Shades and shimmers flickered past her and Héloise stopped fighting for air, breathed out the last of her land self in a stream of bright motes.

The cold stopped hurting, the green dress cleaved to skin, the long wings fusing into fins, her hair clouding the water, leaving a trail of ink.

Below them, Héloise could see city lights, clean and clear, the whole world above recreated below in sharp focus, in echoes and mirrors, and her heart leaped fishbright.

The second of my stories to be printed in the Magazine of Fantasy and Science Fiction. *Another water story, another transformation, another liminal character: a mongrel trying to find their place in the world and finding it only by leaving the world altogether. It's a story about stories, about family histories and secrets. Heloise's vision and the blurred way she saw the world was based on my own, as it's only recently I had an operation that corrected my half blindness.*

About the Author

Cat Hellisen is a writer of dark fantasy for adults and`children. Her work has appeared in Tor.com, *The Magazine of Fantasy and Science Fiction*, and has won the Short Story Day Africa Prize. Her novels include the YA fantasy *When the Sea is Rising Red* and *Beastkeeper*, which she calls a fairy tale for the loveless.

Cat lives in Scotland and decorates her house with Halloween lights because she can. She's terrified of kelp, and really doesn't want to drown.

2001: AN ODYSSEY IN WORDS
Edited by Ian Whates and Tom Hunter

An anthology of original fiction to honour the centenary of Sir Arthur C. Clarke's birth and act as a fund raiser for the Clarke Award. Every story is precisely 2001 words long.

2001 includes stories by 10 winners of the Arthur C. Clarke Award and 13 authors who have been shortlisted, as well as non-fiction by **Neil Gaiman, China Miéville** and Chair of Judges **Andrew M. Butler**.

Cover art by Fangorn

Alastair Reynolds
Bruce Sterling
Gwyneth Jones
Adrian Tchaikovsky
Paul McAuley
Jane Rogers
Ian McDonald
Rachel Pollack
Chris Beckett
Jeff Noon
Colin Greenland
Becky Chambers
Claire North
Dave Hutchinson
Adam Roberts
Yoon Ha Lee
Ian R. MacLeod
Emmi Itäranta
Ian Watson
Liz Williams
& more…

Twenty-seven stories from some of the biggest names in Science Fiction, honouring one of the genre's greats by exploring the limits of imagination.

Released by NewCon Press as a paperback and limited edition hardback.

IMMANION PRESS

Purveyors of Speculative Fiction

www.immanion-press.com

Songs to Earth and Sky edited by Storm Constantine

Some of the best Wraeththu Mythos writers explore the eight seasonal festivals of the year, dreaming up new beliefs and customs, new myths, new dehara – the gods of Wraeththu. As different communities develop among Wraeththu, so fresh legends spring up – or else ghosts from the inception of their kind come back to haunt them. From the silent, snow-heavy forests of Megalithican mountains, through the lush summer fields of Alba Sulh, into the hot, shimmering continent of Olathe, this book explores the Wheel of the Year, bringing its powerful spirits and landscapes to vivid life. The Deharan system of magic explored in these stories reinvents the Pagan Wheel of the Year with an androgynous focus, and will be fascinating both to fans of the Mythos and those who are new to it. Nine brand new tales, including a novella, a novelette and a short story from Storm herself, and stories from *Wendy Darling, Nerine Dorman, Suzanne Gabriel, Fiona Lane* and *E. S. Wynn.* ISBN 978-1-907737-84-8 £11.99 $15.50 pbk

Madame Two Swords by Tanith Lee

An unnamed narrator, in the French city of Troy, finds an old book of the writings of the revolutionary, Lucien de Ceppays, who lived and died in the city two centuries before. She feels a strange bond to the life and thoughts of this long-dead man – what is the mysterious truth behind her obsession? Perhaps she did not find the book at all – perhaps it found her. Some years later, impoverished after the death of her mother, the narrator – in a state of desperation – find herself inexorably guided to meet the peculiar and unnerving Madame Two Swords, an old woman with a history, and her own enduring bonds to Lucien – as well as the book. For the narrator, reality seems to unravel, as she begins to penetrate just how intimately she is connected with Madame Two Swords and Lucien. Previously only available as a limited-edition hardback in 1988, the long-awaited new edition of this vintage-Tanith novella includes illustrations by Jarod Mills. ISBN 978-1-907737-81-7 £11.99, $15.50 pbk

www.ingramcontent.com/pod-product-compliance
Lightning Source LLC
Chambersburg PA
CBHW030124260626
47156CB00008B/2781